FINALLY FREE

THE 707 SERIES
BOOK 3

RILEY EDWARDS

BE A REBEL
Riley Edwards' Romance

Finally Free
The 707 Freedom Series

Cover design: Riley Edwards

Written by: Riley Edwards

Published by: Riley Edwards

Edited by: Cindy Wolken

Finally Free – A Black Ops Romance

First edition – January 2018

This book is dedicated to all the brave men and women who serve or have served in the United States Armed Forces. There are no words to properly convey the sacrifices they make and the appreciation I have for the cost of their service.

To my husband. I wouldn't want anyone else by my side on this crazy train called life.

To my children.

A special thanks to the sailors aboard the USS Nimitz (CVN68). I wrote this series while thinking about her crew, especially my daughter who is currently aboard in support of Operation Inherent Resolve. Welcome home sailors! A job well done! BRAVO ZULU!

To the men in the 3ʳᵈ ID Rock of Marne – **Raider Brigade** *- Fort Stewart, Georgia: As the 1ˢᵗ Armored Brigade Combat Team, 3rd Infantry Division complete their training in preparation for their deployment in support of Operation Resolute Support*

may God be with you as you deploy to Korea. –
Dogface soldiers, CAN DO!

Shades45: Be safe, be brave, and stay strong. We love you and are so proud to call you son. No good-byes only, "See ya laters."

The world lost 31 Heroes 06 Aug 2011. SOC SEAL John W. Faas was among the crew that died that day. Even in death, John continues to inspire all those who knew him and love him. He is not forgotten - never forgotten. His sacrifice and that of his family's reminds us that freedom is never free.

We sleep soundly in our beds because rough men stand ready in the night to visit violence on those who would do us harm.

Whether it was the writer George Orwell, the essayist Richard Grenier, or the Washington Times columnist Rudyard Kipling who originally wrote those words matters not. The sentiment rings true. We are only afforded the luxuries we have because rough men are willing to stand at the ready. Chief Faas was one of those men.

31 heroes – From a grateful nation.

PROLOGUE

Fall 2004

"Holy hell, you see the arm on that boy?" my friend Bee asked.

"Who cares about his arm? That boy is fine," my other friend Lynn said.

"Will both y'all be quiet? Some of us *are trying* to watch the game," I snapped.

There was a minute thirty left on the clock, and Levi McCoy had just thrown a five-yard pass. We were three yards away from winning this game. Virginia might not be as well-known as Texas when it came to football; however, we took our Friday nights during football season real serious around here. The crowd was on their feet and cheering; there was nothin' better than being in the stands watching a game under the lights. It was electrifying. Some Fridays I pulled out my new Motorola baby pink flip phone to record the crowd. I liked to listen to it when I was writing my article for the student paper. The normal spunk of the cheerleaders even seemed to be dialed up for tonight's game. I held my breath when the ball was snapped and Levi caught it, quickly looking for an open receiver. He faked right then took off left, dashing into the end zone when he saw a hole in the defensive line.

"That McCoy is somethin' else. You hear what Kasey said about him?" I guess Lynn hadn't answered fast enough because Bee went on. "They went out last Friday after the game, and *he* went down on *her*. How many juniors you know do that? All the boys I know want *you* to go down on *them*. Not the other way around."

I rolled my eyes at my two idiot friends. As smart as they were, they'd listen to any gossip that came around the bend. And our high school had plenty of it. Just last week I was seen making out with some freshman boy; that was the rumor anyway. It mustn't've been any good, because sure as shit, I couldn't even remember it.

"Blake, you comin' with us to the Tastee-Freez?" Lynn asked.

"Yeah. But I'll hike it home from there. I don't want to tag along to another house party in bum fuck Egypt only to have the troopers bust it ten minutes later."

"Whatever," Lynn mumbled.

We made our way out of the stadium to the student parking lot and piled into Lynn's pickup truck. The Tastee-Freez was already filling up by the time we got there, after stopping at the only convenience store that still accepted fake IDs. Lynn parked her truck next to some of the seniors and jumped out to go talk to them. I dumped my beer into a solo cup and followed Bee to the back of the truck. No sooner was the tailgate down and our asses planted on it, some baseball player that Bee had been tryin' to hook up with jumped up and pushed his way in between Bee and me.

"What the hell?" I muttered.

"Blake, Bee. How are you fine ladies this evenin'?" the guy crooned out.

"Hey, Charlie," Bee gushed. Yes, she gushed, even though it was more in her body language than her tone of voice. She leaned in real close and pushed her impressive boobs into his arm.

I stopped listening to their conversation when a huge black F150 with a modified exhaust that made it so loud it was impossible to ignore pulled into the parking lot. I continued to stare long after the truck's ignition was turned off and the noise had been silenced. I knew who'd be stepping out of the truck; the mystery was which cheerleader would be getting out with him.

Levi McCoy jumped out of the driver's side, freshly showered and dressed in a pair of jeans, black boots, and his normal button up flannel shirt. I would never admit this to anyone, but I'd had a crush on Levi since the first day of our freshman year when we had English class together. Over the years he had gotten bigger, better looking, and better on the football field. Now he looked like a full-grown man and had an ego to match. Even though most of the time he was an arrogant ass, I still couldn't stop crushing on him.

I watched as Levi made his rounds; all the popular kids congratulating him on tonight's win. Fist bumps and guy hugs complete with the back pounding were exchanged. A few girls ran up and kissed his cheek, vying for his attention. It really was interesting how the high school pecking order worked. The jocks were at the top of the pyramid, followed by the rich kids. Those two groups interchanged. It was socially acceptable for a middle-class jock to associate with the wealthy kids that went to our school. But if you were a middle-class no one, such as myself, you'd never be accepted into the popular clique. We didn't dress the same, drive nice cars, and we certainly didn't have the same weekly allowances. Hell, my parents couldn't afford to give me an allowance. I had an afterschool job at the movie theatre.

Bored with people watching and finishing the one beer I could sneak and still go home without my parents noticing, I was about to tell Bee I was leaving when Levi walked up and stopped in front of us.

"Blake, right?" he asked.

I felt my cheeks heat hearing him say my name. I hadn't heard him call me by my name since the first day in English class and that was only because he needed to borrow a pen from me.

"That's me," I stupidly said.

'That's me'; those were my first words I spoke to the boy in almost three full years, not something witty or flirty like one of the cheerleaders would say.

"Thought so. I wanted to tell you I really enjoyed your article in last week's student paper."

I guess he would've liked it. I wrote a two-page spread highlighting his football career at Dominion High School. Scouts were coming around now that he was a junior, trying to get him to early commit to one of their colleges. Rumor had it he was being recruited by five Division I schools, four of those five offering him a full ride if he'd commit. His superior arm gave him a huge advantage over all the other quarterbacks trying to garner the attention of the top schools.

"Glad you liked it. With all your wins it was easy to write. I hope I didn't leave anything out," I responded.

"Oh. The football write-up? That was cool, too. I think you made me sound better than I really am though." Say what? Was Levi McCoy humble? "It's a team effort. I know I get most of the credit, and it isn't fair. Did you know that James Pats has the most receiving yards in the state, and he is on course to beat the Wide Receiver Hall of Fame record?" Levi stopped, and I didn't know what to say. Was he upset I hadn't featured the rest of the team? My assignment was to highlight Levi. "Anyway, I was talking about the student mentoring and tutoring program you're starting. I'd like to volunteer. I can tutor math and science. I'm in AP Bio this semester and AP Calc."

And that was how my relationship with my longtime crush began; me sitting on Lynn's tailgate, an empty solo cup in my hand and a dumbfounded look on my face. He did help me set up the after-school tutoring, and he was an active volunteer. The more time we spent together, the closer we became and the more I got to know the real Levi McCoy, not the star quarterback everyone wanted a piece of. He told me he didn't want a football scholarship; he wanted to join the Army. His dream was to serve his country, not play football. I told him about wanting to be a journalist traveling the world, writing what I saw in faraway places.

The following two years were the best of my life. Even after his mom married Alister Bench, a media mogul, and his family became rich, my relationship with him didn't change. It remained strong despite Levi's wealth. Despite him changing schools. Despite leaving me all by myself. In fact, it allowed me to focus on writing for the student paper, where I became editor.

Life was great.

I was madly in love with the boy of my dreams. A month before graduation, Levi had driven us out to our special hiding spot. It was a secluded wooded area miles outside of town. We went there a lot when we wanted to be alone. It was the very spot I'd given him my virginity the year before. We parked and he swore me to secrecy, telling me he had enlisted in the Army. He had turned eighteen a few weeks before and no longer needed his mother's consent. I was proud that he was following his dreams but scared. After he'd explained everything, he laid me down on a blanket in the grass and made love to me. He told me I had nothing to worry about, that he loved me. After basic training, I would move to where he was stationed and go to college there. We had a plan, a bright and happy future ahead of us.

Everything was perfect until Alister and Levi's mom found out he was leaving for the Army and not going to college to play football. My first mistake was trusting Alister Bench when he called and asked me to come by the house under the pretense he had a letter of recommendation for me to help me get into a summer writing clinic. I should've known something was wrong; the man hated me. He blamed me and my 'low-rent' family for putting 'classless ideas of military service' in Levi's head. I should've smelled the set-up long before I did. Alister quickly ushered me into his study when I arrived at the house. First, he offered me an internship at one of his newspapers if I would break up with Levi and tell him to scrap his military plans. When that didn't work, he offered me money, lots of it. He offered to pay for my college, pay off my parents' house, and buy me a car. The gifts he was willing to give were endless. The man was desperate for me to leave Levi. Through it all, my mind and heart never wavered. I allowed him to continue to bribe me. At eighteen-years-old I thought I could play with the big wig and win. Boy was I wrong. Just when I thought I had everything I needed to bring Alister Bench down the front door slammed shut.

That door ended up being a lot more than a rectangular piece of wood. It was my future, and it was lost to me. All the plans we had made, the love we had shared, all the hope I had of one day marrying Levi, crashed shut that afternoon. Every phone call, text message, every letter I wrote Levi while he was in basic training went unanswered. A few months after he should've graduated basic, his phone was disconnected.

He was gone.

My freshman year of college I made a promise to myself. One day, somehow, someway, I would destroy Alister Bench.

CHAPTER ONE

Levi

"We have a situation," the commander announced when he entered the hangar.

I turned in my chair to find Clark already at the large conference room style table and the commander moving toward him with a stack of folders in his arms.

"What'd we miss?" Jasper asked, as he and Lenox walked in.

"Nothing yet," Clark answered, and hit the remote to turn the fifty-two-inch monitor on the wall along with several smaller screens.

"Levi, pull up SAT one niner Zulu on the big screen," the commander ordered.

I turned back to my computer, and with a few

clicks, I had live drone footage of Yemen's capital city up on the screen.

"Earlier today an American investigative reporter was captured in a small village fifty kilometers east of Sana'a," the commander explained. "Latest intel shows the caravan headed to the city."

"Anyone claiming responsibility?" I asked.

"Yes, a group that calls themselves the Liberty Revolution, a radical Christian group," the commander answered, using his tablet to pull up a photograph on one of the smaller screens. "Ahmed Al-Harazi is the leader. He began his crusade eighteen months ago, trying to spread Christianity through the outer villages."

"How does he go from spreading Christianity to kidnapping a journalist?" Clark asked.

"Six months ago, a jihadist group bombed one of his churches and the surrounding village. Ninety-three people were killed. After the attack, his message changed. He went from spreading the word of God to an avenging extremist, using the Bible as his weapon and putting his own spin on an eye for an eye."

"He forgot the 'turn the other cheek' part," Jasper muttered. "Why haven't we heard of them?"

"They're only five-hundred strong tops. Most of

his followers deflected after the church bombing, fearing that if they were found out to be Christians, they'd die as well." The commander changed the image on the screen to a hooded figure, small in stature with their hands tied in front of their body.

I looked closer at the image. "Is that a woman?" I asked.

"Yes. Blake Porter. She is the journalist. She was embedded sixty days ago investigating Al-Harazi and the Liberty Revolution."

"Come again?" I spit out, hoping that I hadn't heard the lying scheming bitch's name I had been trying to forget since the summer after I graduated high school.

"Blake Porter, she is the lead investigative reporter for the Daily Sun."

Sure enough, I'd heard correctly.

"You've heard of her?" Clark asked.

"Something like that," I answered. With a nod, Clark turned back to the monitors, dropping his line of questioning.

"Is there an evac plan in place?" Jasper inquired. He and Lenox had rolled a topographical map of Yemen out over the table.

"Mission specifics are in your briefs. The objective is a clean in-and-out rescue. The President would like to have this contained before news hits the wire. The national security advisor does not want to give this group any media time. We have forty-eight hours before Porter's next scheduled check-in with the paper. If she misses that call in, the Daily Sun will contact government officials and run a story."

"Copy that," Lenox said.

"Wheels up in thirty, ladies. Good luck." The commander walked out of the hangar, giving us time to gear up.

"Give me five to call Lily," Lenox said, grabbing his cell.

"You better call Emily and let her know. I'll grab your kit," I told Jasper.

Things had changed a lot around the 707 in the last year. First Lenox and Lily, and now Jasper and Emily. The women were a welcomed addition to the family. It was good seeing both of my brothers in love, especially Jasper. He'd carried a burden that was not his to bear for a long time. I was happy he had finally made peace with his daughter's death. As pleased as I was for them, there was a twinge of something in my gut. With two of the four of us married off, or almost married in Jasper's case, it made a man re-evaluate what he wanted out of life.

Before Lily and Emily came along, I was content being single. I figured that would be my life until I left the 707. The possibility of a family never crossed my mind. The team had lived for the thrill of the hunt and the adrenaline rush when we were closing in on a target. Now, they had something more important to live for. Family. I'd cut mine out of my life a long time ago, the same day I left Blake. I was better off without them. After my mom married Alister Bench, she became a different person than she was when she was raising my sister and me on a waitress's salary. We didn't have much, but we had each other. Once she married Alister, she turned into a trophy wife, and my sister finally got to join the cool crowd clique she'd desperately wanted to be a part of.

Alister had bought every person I had ever loved, including Blake. That had been the final knife in my back.

"All straight?" Clark called out from the cage.

He walked out of the enclosure with four M4 carbines slung over his shoulder and two ammo cans. I hadn't realized that I still hadn't moved until he spoke.

"Five by five," I answered and went about grabbing the rest of the gear.

By the time we heard the helo blades outside we were ready to go. We'd be transported by helicopter to DC where we'd catch a flight to Yemen with the Air Force. While commercial flights were more comfortable, the paper trail hauling a weapons cache overseas left an electronic footprint we didn't want. We didn't exist. We were a four-man unit the Army classified as research and development. As far as anyone knew, including our fellow soldiers, we procured and tested new weapons. We also oversaw the armories and made sure weapons were checked back in after a battalion deployed. We did test weapons, just not the way the Army thought. Our testing was done on secret covert black ops. We were personal assassins for the President, or in this case, rescuing a hostage our government didn't want the world to know was captured.

The flight to Andrews was quiet, each of us going over the SITREP the commander had left. As hard as I tried not to read Blake's bio and personal file, I couldn't stop myself. Twelve years ago, I'd walked out of my stepfather's house and shut the door to my past. I'd promised myself I would never look back, never allow another person to use me again. Even after all these years, I could still feel the sting of the blade as Blake stabbed me in the back. I'd never expected it from her. I'd thought she loved me as much as I'd loved her. Stupidly I had been walking around with a promise ring in my pocket for weeks, waiting for the right time to give it to her. A promise that one day I would ask her to be my wife. She was smart and funny. And damn was she beautiful; the classic girl next door, sugar all the way through.

I'd taken my time getting to know her. She'd been different from all the other girls I'd been with. She wasn't one of the cheerleaders that wanted to bag Levi McCoy, the quarterback, for bragging rights. Not that it was worth bragging about anyway. When she'd started to push for me to go further, I'd refused. Blake was sweet and shy and had never been with a boy. I wanted to go slow and show her she was special. I'd spent months getting her ready for sex. I wanted her first time to be perfect, something we'd both never forget. That was the problem, I couldn't forget. I couldn't forget the way she looked at me with love and lust swirling in her pretty hazel orbs. I couldn't forget what it felt like when I entered her the first time, pushing through her virginity. I remembered it all like it happened yesterday. To this day, I also remembered the searing pain of her betrayal.

Now, here I was, all these years later, flying halfway around the world to save the woman who crushed my soul. The irony wasn't lost on me. The only sliver of satisfaction I would gain from this rescue mission was that she would have to see every-thing she'd tossed away. I hoped that my stepfather's money was worth it.

The C-17 Globemaster was already on the tarmac waiting for our departure when we landed at Andrews. I had fifteen hours to get my head on straight and prepare to see the only woman I had ever loved.

Ain't life a bitch.

CHAPTER TWO

Blake

"Sir, I don't understand what you want me to do."

That was a lie. I knew full well what the man in the suit across the table from me wanted. Not that I'd give him the pleasure of admitting it. I was going to sit here as long as possible and play dumb. The men who'd yanked me out of my tent and taken me had already deleted all of my electronic backups. Mr. White, as he called himself, made a show of deleting every file I had saved in my cloud storage. He even went as far as wiping every fake email address clean of data. It was as though I had never written a single word. I was beyond pissed. Pissed was in the rearview mirror and I'd skated into thermonuclear.

All the information I'd gathered on Al-Harazi was gone. With a few keystrokes, Mr. White and his men had rendered me dead in the water. My only hope was some of my work would be saved on the Daily Sun's servers. If not, I was screwed.

"I think you understand perfectly well, Ms. Porter. We are politely asking you not to run a story in the name of national security," the man repeated.

"Mr. White, you keep saying that. However, what you're failing to explain is how a humanitarian piece on the village will somehow be a matter of national security. Since when is clean drinking water a threat to the nation?" I asked.

I had been careful in the information I kept on my computer and what I spoke about over the phone to my editor. There was no way this man could know the real reason I was in Yemen. Everything had been kept off the record. Unless...

"Are you really going to insult my intelligence? We both know you're here for information on the Liberty Revolution."

Well shit.

"Who?" I asked, praying that all my years of playing dumb to look as non-threatening as possible would pay off.

Mr. White tilted his head and stared at me as if I

wasn't innocent at all. I was merely stupid to try and lie to him. I wasn't stupid. I knew a company man when I saw one. The CIA had sent in a team to neutralize me and scrub my records. The real question here was how did the CIA get involved? My mission objective was off the books. Only one person was supposed to know I was here.

"Tell me, Mr. White, how exactly did you come about my location," I asked, tiring of the game.

The funny thing about covert ops is we both had an idea who the other person worked for, but neither of us would confirm it. Instead, we both sat staring at one another in some sort of standoff. I knew it was a matter of time before my backup arrived. It was a waiting game; none of the Mr. Whites or Mr. Blues in the room would kill me, or they would've done it already. They didn't have the kill order; they only wanted my intel. None of it was on any computer they had found. Now, Mr. White was on a fact-finding mission to see how much I knew. I knew a whole hell of a lot, none of which I would tell him.

"How long are we going to have to do this before you tell me the information I need, and we can both go home?" he asked.

"Considering you hold the key to walking us

both out of here and you don't seem real eager, I'd say another ten hours at least."

"Ten hours? Why ten hours Special Agent?"

I allowed a wide smile to play across my lips. "Good guess, but no dice. For a spook, you're not all that smart. I don't have anything to tell you. You're wasting your time."

"Why ten hours?" he asked again.

I didn't answer, and Mr. White spent the next few hours sitting across a makeshift table from me in a grungy room, eating his lunch. If he thought the temptation of food would make me talk, he was sorely mistaken. I had gone far longer than the twentyish hours since they'd taken me without food or water. This was a cakewalk – the lap of luxury as far as captivity was concerned. My job had taken me all over the world, some of the vilest places the earth had to offer. If Mr. CIA man thought he was going to break me with a staring contest, he was wrong.

The door to the interrogation room flew open. Two men dressed in black, their faces fully concealed, came into view; their M4s up and at the ready before Mr. White could draw his sidearm.

"Three more in the main building," I advised.

"Affirmative. They're down," one of the men said.

"Shit. They're CIA." I lowered my head and sighed. "Mr. White, I tried to tell you we should've parted ways."

"Figured that much when they had no weapons and creds out the moment we breached. Someone wanna fill us in on why my team is here to rescue a reporter from the agency?" the man asked looking at Mr. White.

"I'd like to know the same thing, but Mr. White has been less than forthcoming. Maybe you'll have better luck. I have a deadline to make, and this little stunt has put me behind. My editor won't be happy."

I stood, thinking now was the perfect time to get gone. Let the men fight it out amongst themselves.

"You, sit," the second man ordered. Chills raced up my spine, and all the fine hairs on my arms stood on end despite the heat in the room.

I narrowed my eyes at the man; there was something about his voice that was familiar. "Excuse me?" I asked.

"You heard me, sit down," the man commanded. "And Mr. White, Brown, Jones whatever fucking name you're using this time, I suggest you start talking. I have a feeling we're being led around by our dicks, and I'm not real fond of the spy shit. I like things clear and precise. I want to look a man in the face when I kill him, not play games and stab him in the back like a coward."

With every word the man spoke my heart rate spiked. Not once while I was being detained was I afraid; now that I recognized the voice I was petrified.

Levi McCoy.

The only man I had ever loved. The man whose stepfather I would one day ruin. I wasn't ready to see him. Not now, and not this way. I was so close to finishing my mission.

"Sorry to drag you all the way here under false pretense, but there was no other way. I knew the Director of National Intelligence would only send in your team to recover his golden child. There was no other way," Mr. White said.

"No other way for what? Did the commander know?" Levi's friend asked.

"Let's all sit down, and I'll fill you in. One of you will have to convince the *reporter* to hand over her latest intel to confirm my lead. She has proven to be stubborn," Mr. White said, sounding exasperated I wouldn't roll over like he wanted.

Tough tits. No one was getting any intel I had. I was the lowly reporter here. At least that was my story, and I was sticking to it.

"Did you try bending her over your knee and spanking her?" Levi asked. "I heard it was quite effective on Ms. Porter."

Bastard.

I tried to remain emotionless, not allowing a single muscle on my face to move. "That hasn't worked for a very long while, Levi. Please, take the mask off and stay awhile. We have a lot to catch up on. Seems you've made the jump from cavalry scout to black ops."

The man standing next to Levi didn't flinch when I said Levi's name or announced there was familiarity. He was trained well; he gave nothing away. Levi wasn't as disciplined; he was uncomfortable. I would need him off balance if I had any chance of leaving here with my sanity.

"Clark," Mr. White started. "I didn't know. I had no idea Ms. Tight-lips and Levi had a past. I only need to pass along intel. I need you personally to give it to the director."

"Do I look like a goddamn carrier pigeon? Fly back and give it to him yourself," the man, who I assumed was Clark, argued.

"This has been fun. But I think you men should work this out. I really need to make my deadline. I don't have anything for you. May I please go?" I asked in the sweetest voice I could muster.

While it was interesting to watch the men argue, I had shit to do and deadlines to meet. I was hours behind schedule and would have to pay double to get across the border now that the locals had seen me be taken hostage.

"Fuck," Levi growled and pulled off the black balaclava that had been covering his handsome face.

I'll be damned.

Levi McCoy had aged well. He hadn't actually aged; he'd just gotten better looking. The beautiful teenage star football player had turned into a sexy mercenary. It was time for me to leave. His voice sent chills racing through my body, and seeing his face was making me burn all over.

God, I had missed him all these years.

"Someone better start talking," Clark demanded.

I was no longer paying attention to the questions being asked. I couldn't take my eyes off Levi. The last time I had actually seen him, he was dropping me off at my house with a long kiss at my door. That was after he had spent hours kissing other parts of my body. I could still remember what it felt like to be loved by Levi.

It had been everything.

CHAPTER THREE

Levi

She looked the same, but different. Her teenage body had filled out, her breasts looked larger, her hips had a gentle flare, and her once light brown hair was now lighter. Maybe chemically highlighted, but by the look of it, I would guess sun bleached from months in the desert. She was still stunning, and still a lying bitch. I would do well to remember that the first time around she had no issue with knifing me in the back.

"Porter was embedded sixty days ago, her cover was as a reporter trying to get an exclusive interview with Al-Harazi," Mr. White explained.

"Her cover?" I asked. I read her file. Blake started

at the Daily Sun after she graduated college and had been there the last eight years.

"Blake Porter works directly for the Director of National Intelligence." Mr. White turned to look at Blake. "She is a deep cover agent." Blake sat quietly, her face completely blank, not confirming or denying what Mr. White said. "Without her knowledge, the director sent my team in as her back up. The region is too hot not to have someone on standby for a quick EXFIL if she needed." Still nothing from Blake. Completely stone-faced. She had perfected her con. She was a good liar when she'd screwed me over; I hadn't seen it coming. But this was exceptional. "There was word that Al-Harazi was planning his exit. At the last minute, he added another passenger and a woman's cover. He was planning on taking Porter with him to Oman."

"So, you took her before Al-Harazi could," I concluded.

"Do you have anything to add, Ms. Porter?" Clark asked.

"Please, call me Blake. Nothing at all," she replied.

Her thumbnail was slowly scraping the tip of her pointer finger. That was her tell. When she was nervous about something, she always rubbed her fingers together. Other than that, her body language was soft, unassuming, and relaxed.

I turned back to Mr. White, "What else? There had to be more than a planned kidnapping to call in a rescue mission. The CIA already had Blake safely away from Al-Harazi; you could've packed it up and gone home."

"Six months ago, Al-Harazi blew up one of his churches and blamed a jihadist group who was more than happy to take the credit for killing a bunch of Christians," Mr. White continued. "He wanted an excuse to turn his followers into extremists. What better way than improvise an attack on your own people. He's planning on blowing up nineteen embassies, including the U.S.'s in Muscat, Oman. I believe he was bringing Blake along to draw American soldiers into a trap."

That got Blake's attention. Her lip twitched ever so slightly, and her cheeks were turning rosy. The dreaded blush. A person could learn to control just about any response, but there are some that were harder than others. Learning to slow your body's response so you don't flush is a hard skill to master. She almost had it, but it was too late.

"Why not call it in?" I asked.

"I did. I had no hard evidence. I needed the

recordings Blake had to confirm before the call would be made to bring your team in," he explained.

"You have her, why didn't you just take it from her?" I asked.

"I tried. She's smart; she doesn't have it on her person, and it was not on any of the secured networks."

The side of Blake's mouth tipped up for a split second before she covered it up. Poor Mr. White was just now learning what I had known the past twelve years; she was a sneaky bitch.

"Where is it, Blake?" I asked.

She shrugged her shoulders. "It's been really fun sitting here chatting with you all, and all of this is going to be great for my story. But frankly, I'm bored. And I've done nothing wrong. You have no reason to detain me. I'm leaving now." Blake stood and squared her shoulders.

"You're gonna let nineteen embassies be bombed? You really haven't changed; you're still the cold-hearted bitch you've always been."

"Think whatever you'd like Levi. You've always jumped to conclusions. It's your biggest downfall. You make decisions based on emotion instead of facts. Nice to see that you haven't changed either." She stopped and turned to Mr. White. "If any of your men try and stop me, I will shoot them, agency or not. I will not be as nice as the men. I have a job to do, one that you thoroughly fucked up. Next time you think you know something, remember you don't. I answer to one man. I have my orders, and this little stunt you just pulled might have just caused thousands of deaths."

"You knew Al-Harazi planned on taking you," I guessed.

"Of course, I did. Where do you think he got his intel?" She stopped and pointed at Mr. White. "He was piggybacking off of mine. I will be having a long talk with the director when I get back about who he sends in as back up. I don't need it, I don't want it, and this cluster fuck of crap proves that."

"And what did you have planned once he kidnapped you? He wasn't going to put you up in the Four Seasons. He would've tortured you, maybe even killed you. Then he would've continued on to blow up three city blocks, Blake," I all but yelled.

"You really are dense. This isn't my first rodeo, football star. He would've never made it that far," she said, squaring her shoulders.

"You had the kill order," Clark interjected.

If it were anyone else in front of me, I would've told them it was a good plan. Dangerous, but good.

"Well, that plan is shot to hell. You and the super spy squad will be on your way stateside in a few hours, and my team will take it from here," I said.

Gone was the composed well-trained agent. Blake's face turned a deep shade of red, and she exploded.

"The hell you will. This is my op. I will not be thrown off because some overzealous agent decided it was time to call in the men. I have everything covered. Two months I worked to get Al-Harazi to trust me. I have shown a despicable man kindness and understanding in order to get close. Do you have any idea how hard it is to agree with a man that I know killed innocent people? When I know what he is planning? Every time that man touches me I want to vomit, but I suck it up knowing that I will get the pleasure of slicing his throat before he carries out one of the largest bombings in recent history."

I will admit, I was a little turned on by her outburst and a whole lot pissed. "You let that man touch you?" I spit out.

"That's what you have to say? There you go again, allowing your emotions to override your common sense. What I do to get close to a mark is none of your business, and I will not sit here and listen to any more of this bullshit. I have a mission to complete. Get the fuck out of my way."

"There is zero chance you're doing this on your own," Clark interjected. "You might have your orders, but I have mine. And mine are to bring you home safe and sound."

"I'm sorry, Blake. I didn't get confirmation that you had been briefed on the kidnapping plot," Mr. White apologized.

Blake's face softened when she looked at him, and that, too, pissed me off. "I know you didn't. I wasn't briefed because it was *my* intel. I get it, wires get crossed, and split-second decisions have to be made. I understand you thought you were doing the right thing. The issue I have is instead of treating me like a fellow operative you treated me like a damsel in distress. Then you sat here wasting hours playing agency games instead of recognizing I'm your equal. Now, I need to rush my timeline and pray that the convoy hasn't left me behind. Al-Harazi might think twice about trying to take me now. I'm sure word got out that an American reporter was taken. Everyone, please, I have a chance to save this op," Blake pleaded.

"Clark, sorry to interrupt, command called. There's been a mission shift. Blake Porter is to be released. Mr. White," Jasper stopped and pointed at the CIA agent in the room, "Stays with us as backup and the rest of the rainbow in the other room are to fall back and stay here."

"Copy that," Clark answered. "If you're staying you need another name. There is not a chance in fuck I'm calling you Mr. White or any other spy name. If you don't want to give me your real name, make one up. Harry, Frank, James, I don't care. Anything is better than Mr. White."

"Grayson," Mr. White answered.

"Seriously? So, what, your nickname is Gray? What is wrong with you spooks?" I asked.

"Take it up with my mom. That's the name she gave me," he answered.

"When was the last time you had contact with Al-Harazi?" Clark asked Blake.

"I don't know? What day is it?" she asked.

"We've had her twenty-two hours. Her last contact was about an hour before my team went in," Grayson answered.

Blake had sat back down, her cunning eyes taking in the room. She was formulating a plan of escape.

"If you run, I will find you. Don't get any ideas in that pretty little head of yours."

"As if you would. I could walk right out the door, slam it so hard the building shook, and you'd never even bother. You'd turn your back; it's what you're good at. It normally comes right after one of your emotional fits."

Fuck me, the woman knew where to sucker punch.

"One tends to walk away when he learns the woman he was planning on marrying would rather take his daddy's money than have to slum it. Don't worry baby; there's been no shortage of women who didn't mind having to slum it over the years. Hope dear old dad came through on all those big promises. Tell me, did his check clear? God knows there were an awful lot of zeros at the end."

Blake's face paled and hurt flashed in her eyes. There was a moment of guilt thick in my gut, but the moment she masked her pain the guilt fled just as fast. She was a master of deception, especially now that she had been trained by the CIA.

She couldn't be trusted.

CHAPTER FOUR

Blake

You would've thought that after all these years his words wouldn't have hurt me. And maybe they wouldn't have if I'd been able to stop loving him. He'd very obviously been able to. He thought I had taken Alister's money and he turned all the love we had for each other into hate. I didn't have that luxury. I knew the truth. I couldn't even be angry at him for walking out on me. I should've hated him for not returning my calls, or not writing me back, but I couldn't muster the courage to do it. If I stopped loving him, it was like everything I had been trying to do the last twelve years was for nothing.

Every lead I tracked down, all the money trails I followed, will have been for nothing. Well, that was not entirely true. There was a bonus in operation: *bury Alister Bench*. I took down the men he gave money to and the terrorist organizations he funded. Bench had funneled a million dollars to Al-Harazi through various charities. That million dollars was now going to be used to bomb three city blocks. The yin and yang. I was plotting revenge and murder yet doing good for the world in the process.

"As much as I love a good soap opera, we have a new mission to plan," Clark said. "When is Al-Harazi planning on crossing into Oman?"

"Three hours," I told him. "I will have just enough time if I leave now."

"No, you won't. Change of plans. We'll use Grayson's fuck up to our advantage. You and I will go to Al-Harazi and ask him for safe passage into Oman," Levi suggested.

"No way. It won't work. I have to go alone."

The thought of having to spend any more time with Levi made my stomach turn, and my heart ache. I had to concentrate on taking out my mark, not remembering every sweet thing Levi ever said to me.

"It will work. It is the perfect plan. Al-Harazi knows that you were taken. Levi can be your cover; he helped you escape, now you both need passage. Offer him money to take you across the border. If he wants you as badly as you say he does, he'll want to help you. This way he can look at himself as your savior. He'll think you're grateful to him, making you easier to control," Clark added.

"Sure, and Levi doesn't reek of American soldier? He's even dressed the part. Al-Harazi will smell that a mile away, and kill us both. No thanks. I'll go in alone; that's the plan."

I had to admit, the idea was good and maybe if any of the other guys had offered to go, I might have considered it.

"That was the old plan, welcome to the new one. He'll change clothes with one of the *Rainbow Brites* and play the part of a businessman held for ransom. It's not like that is a far stretch in Yemen," Clark continued.

"And the lack of beard and any bruising from the beating he would've taken?" I asked.

"Easy. He was taken the same time you were, twenty-four hours ago. And it wouldn't be the first time we had to stage a fight to leave some marks."

This was not going as planned. Clark had an answer to every question I threw out. And if I asked one of the other men to accompany me it would tip my hand and show more than I wanted them to see. I wanted Levi to believe I was just as unaffected as he was; that having him standing in front of me wasn't giving me butterflies in my belly and flashbacks of my youth. I was a trained killer, a professional, not some silly school girl with a crush.

"Two is one, and one is none. You know it's better to have backup with you," Levi said. I think that was the first time he had spoken to me like I was a person and not scum on the bottom of his shoe.

They were right. My original plan was shot to shit, and I'd need some explanation as to how I'd escaped so quickly.

"What do I need to know about your cover?" I asked.

"Nothing. You don't know me. I'll make the rest up on the fly. If we run into trouble and we need to abort just ask me 'Do you have family back home?' If one of us asks that we'll know it's time to bug out."

"Okay."

"Jasper and Lenox will go ahead of us to Muscat. Grayson and I will be behind you," Clark explained.

There was no point in continuing to argue; he was coming with me. I needed to pull my shit together and get my head back on the op instead of staring at Levi. Even in his tactical gear, I could make out how much bigger and broader he'd grown since I'd last seen him. I wanted to study him, ask him questions, hear his voice, see his smile, but none of that was going to happen. He hated me, and I had a mission to complete.

"Grayson, change clothes with me. You're the closest to my size." Levi didn't wait for Grayson's answer before he walked out the door leaving me in the room alone with Clark.

"So, you're the one?" he asked.

"The one what?" I wasn't entirely sure what he was asking.

"The one that got away."

What the hell did he say? The one that got away? More like the one that was tossed out on her ass like yesterday's trash.

"I don't know what he's told you about me but I'm not what he says I am," I tried to explain.

"He hasn't told me a damn thing."

"Then why would you say that?" I asked.

"There is only one thing that can gut a man and crush his soul. A woman," Clark declared.

"He doesn't look crushed to me."

And he didn't. He looked strong and capable, like he was comfortable in his role being a soldier. I always knew he'd fit in and do well. I was proud of him. He had followed his dream and done exactly what he'd set out to do. He turned down every scholarship that was offered to him, and he followed his heart.

"Looks can be deceiving. I don't know what happened between the two of you, and I don't much care. I do know on this op I'm in charge. Today, for the duration, I'm the one man you answer to, and Levi is in charge of you in the field."

White hot rage coursed through my veins. The arrogance of this prick. For eight long years, I've been putting up with a double standard being a woman. I was sick as shit of always having to prove my worth.

Without thinking, I was over the table, and my right hand found his blade in the sheath on his left hip. A split second later the tip of the cool metal was pressed against his throat.

"Looks *can* be deceiving. You underestimate my skill and my usefulness. I will not be treated like a delicate flower that needs protecting. I have just as much experience in the field as you do."

I looked to the doorway, both Levi and Grayson staring at me with either appreciation in their eyes, or they thought I'd lost my shit. Either way, I didn't care.

"Glad to hear it," Clark said and smiled. He took advantage of my hesitation, knocking the knife out of my hand and twisting me around. "Now tell me,

Blake. Would you like an open slap or a closed fist?" he chuckled.

Well damn, this was the part of the job I hated the most. Being hit. But it was necessary. For us to pull off that I'd been taken and held hostage, I had to have marks too.

"I'll take a fist. I hate being slapped like a bitch," I answered.

"Noted." Clark let go of me, and I turned to face him. "I'll pull it as much as I can, just enough to leave a mark. Turn your face a little; I don't want to break your cheek."

"I'm fine. I told you, I've been in the field a long time. I've taken a hit a time or two, and *they* were not pulling their punches."

I turned my head and braced myself for the pain. There was a loud crack and pain radiated from the side of my face followed by a growl from across the room.

"That will never happen again," Levi roared.

My hand flew to the side of my face, and I sucked in air. Holy shit that hurt, and it took me a moment to be able to speak. When I finally could, I turned to Levi. "Oh, come on, the sight of a little punch to the face bothers you? For a big bad commando, you sure are squeamish," I taunted, trying to break the tension in the room. I didn't want to begin to process why Levi was so mad.

"You think you're funny Blake. Fuck you." Levi stormed out of the room, and a moment later there was a loud bang, then another. It sounded like Levi was punching a wall.

Clark sighed. "One of those idiots better get him under control before he breaks his knuckles. You still think he doesn't look crushed? Levi is the coolest operator I have, the most calculating and precise. That man in there has lost his ever-loving mind."

I remained quiet. I didn't know what to say. I had a mission to complete, and I didn't have time to deal with Levi's temper tantrum. Even if I did, he wouldn't talk to me. He had refused to speak to me for twelve years. A few minutes later the sickening sound of a fist hitting flesh could be heard from the other room. Someone was working him over pretty good.

Levi would need more marks than me. Male prisoners were treated worse than the women. I could get away with a single mark on my face. Levi couldn't.

When he finally reentered the room, I had to force myself to stay planted. I wanted to run to him and tend to his bloodied face. He looked horrible.

"If you broke my nose, Jasper, I'm gonna kick your ass when we get home," Levi grumbled before he turned to me. "You ready?" he asked.

"Yeah. Grayson, is there any of my equipment left or did you clean it all?" I asked.

"Everything has been scrubbed," he said.

Asshole. He at least had the decency to look sorry.

"Burn it before you go. I'd take it out myself, but I don't have time. At least give me back my cell. I don't know if I'll be allowed to keep it, but I'd like to try. It's clean, so if I have to toss it, it won't be a problem.

Grayson pulled my phone out of his pocket, along with my press credentials and passport and handed them to me.

"We'll ditch the car and huff it the last three miles back to the village right before the security checkpoint," I told the men. "My next check-in is in twenty-four hours with evac instructions. I assume you will handle that call to the DNI. If we get separated, my rally point is a small dock behind the British embassy, but let's hope it doesn't get to that point."

"The director has been alerted to the new play. Levi, you stay on Blake. We will track your movements using your chip. I hate that we won't have comms. Be safe, and I'll catch you on the flip side." Clark gave Levi a fist bump and turned to me. "Remember you're not alone; use your backup if you need it."

I fought the urge to roll my eyes. Everyone in the room treated me like I was wet behind the ears.

"Copy that." I turned to Levi. "Let's roll."

I hoped I sounded stronger than I felt. My hands were shaking as I shoved my belongings into the pocket of my pants and clipped the knife, the only weapon I would have until it was taken from me again, inside of the waistband.

Levi and I slipped out the back door and found a car to hotwire. Fifty kilometers was too far to walk; as guilty as I felt for stealing a car, it was necessary. Naturally, Levi slipped into the driver's seat even though I knew the area better.

"Where to?" he asked.

"I can drive, you know?" I sassed.

"Yeah, that's great. Where to?"

This was going to be a long couple of days. If Al-Harazi didn't kill me on the spot, having to be up close and personal with Levi would.

CHAPTER FIVE

Levi

I hated to admit it, but Blake was sexy as hell when she jumped over the table and pulled Clark's knife on him. I knew it was a test. Clark enjoyed putting someone new through the paces; however, that test was out of necessity, to see if Blake was competent. I was actually impressed she was able to pull Clark's blade as quickly as she did. Twelve years had definitely changed her. The old Blake could cut a person down to size using her impressive vocabulary, not jump a table. The old Blake closed her eyes during horror movies and thought that *The Bourne Supremacy* was too violent. The new Blake seemed to have gotten a handle on her disgust of blood. She took Clark's hit like a pro, barely flinching when his fist made contact with her face. What the hell had she been up to over the years? The sight of Clark hitting her, no matter how necessary it was, made me see red. I knew he'd pulled the punch; he didn't want to hurt her any more than I wanted to see it. However, it didn't make a damn bit of difference to me. I still wanted to kick his ass for touching her.

Blake's directions maneuvered us through the streets of Sana'a and out of the city. A long dirt trail lay ahead of us.

"How did you get recruited?" I asked.

I needed something to fill the awkward silence; anything to stop my mind from going back to a time I've tried to forget, a time where the love of my life gutted me for money and power.

"I was in college. I showed potential and was approached my junior year. I went through the selection process and began training when I passed my psychological exams."

"I'm surprised someone as well adjusted as you could pass the psych evals. The CIA tends to like to recruit people who have questionable morals, and will easily push morality aside for the greater good."

Blake was the kindest person I knew. It was hard to believe that the studious girl I knew could begin to pass as a field agent. An analyst, sure. She was definitely smart enough.

"Funny what a person with nothing left to lose is willing to do for the greater good. Besides, it was purely selfish on my part. Joining the CIA had personal gains for me. I needed their resources. They saw a void in me that needed to be filled, and I allowed them to believe they were exploiting it," she explained.

I wasn't going to touch that with a ten-foot pole. *She* had nothing to lose? I guess not, she hadn't lost it in the first place; she threw it away.

"How long have you been in the field?" I inquired.

"What the hell is this? The Spanish Inquisition?" She continued to look out her window, refusing to look in my direction.

As much as it hurt when her pretty eyes were cast my way, I would rather have the pain than her indifference. I was the injured party here, not her, yet she acted like I'd wronged her and she couldn't look at me.

"I'm trying to figure out how closely I'm going to have to watch your ass so we both don't get dead," I lied.

Jasper had a full workup of Blake Porter once we

figured out she worked for the National Intelligence Office. I didn't have time to read the entire brief, but I did see she had several accommodations and awards. She was well respected in her office and by the director himself. In eight years she seemed to have moved up the chain fairly quickly.

"I've been in the field long enough to smell bull-shit, Levi. I know that one of your men pulled my jacket. I know you read it. I knew that Mr. White was agency before he pulled the hood off my head and I saw a suit standing in front of me. Kidnappings are not gentle in this country, and the man didn't have it in him to manhandle me. If I had thought for one second I was truly being taken, he would have been dead the moment the flap in my tent rustled when he entered. I think the question is, how closely will I have to watch you on this op? You're used to your men at your six. I work alone. I'm used to slipping in and out. I don't need someone at my back when I cut a man's throat." Blake called me on my bullshit.

"What makes you think I read your file?"

"Because I would've if I were you. You have the advantage. You know I'm capable of handling myself. I wasn't given the same courtesy and allowed to read your file. So, Levi McCoy, how long have *you* been in the field?" she asked, turning the tables.

I drove in silence for a moment thinking about how much I was willing to tell her. I didn't want Blake to know anything about my life. But she was right on one account; she did deserve to know who her partner was on a mission.

"About ten years now. The first two years of my service were tied up in training." That small amount of information was all I was willing to share.

Blake remained quiet, and I couldn't help but wonder what had changed so drastically for her that she would give up her dream of being a journalist to join the CIA. I guess she still got to live part of her dream, her long-standing cover was a journalist, but it was with a newspaper that was run by the CIA. I wondered if she actually got to write real articles about the faraway places she got to see. That was what Blake had always wanted to do. She wanted her words to impact people's lives. When I walked out of my stepfather's house, I followed my dreams. I became exactly the man I'd always knew I would become. I had everything I'd ever wanted, minus the woman I thought would be by my side.

Her life had taken a sharp left turn. I wanted to ask if her parents were okay. If something tragic had happened to one of them, I could see how that would derail her plans. Short of that, I couldn't figure out why she wasn't a reporter somewhere, married to a regular Joe Blow with a couple of kids running around. Shit, maybe she was married. I hadn't read that part of her file. And even though I had access to any information I could ever want, I'd never looked her up. I admit there had been times over the years when I missed her so much I had thought about it. Then I remembered what the pain of her betrayal felt like and I didn't do it.

"Bravo One. You're coming up on the checkpoint," Clark said in my ear.

"Copy that, Bravo Two," I returned. "Did you have a spot you wanted to ditch the car?" I asked Blake.

"There will be a cut off on the left. We can walk the last three miles. There is plenty of cover on the east side," Blake told me.

"Did you hear that?" I asked Clark.

"Copy. There will be a SWCC boat at the dock should you need a water evac. Chalk 1 will be on standby for your extraction point, five klicks due east of the American Embassy. Red smoke will call your ride. Remember Columbia?" Clark chuckled.

"How could I forget."

The team had barely made it out of that mission alive. The helo was lifting off, and both Clark and I had grabbed the ladder to evac. Our asses were swinging in the wind until we could safely climb aboard.

"Let's not repeat that, friend."

"Roger that. Bravo One, out."

I pulled my earpiece out preparing to destroy my communication device. From here on out we'd be black. Blake and I would have to work together as a team to take out Al-Hazari.

"A SWCC team has been deployed to the dock," I explained the exit plan to Blake. She had to know as well. If I didn't make it, she'd need to know where to go. When I was done explaining where the Special Warfare Combatant-Craft Crew would be, she nodded her head.

"Good to know we'll have a SEAL team in place if shit goes sideways. I plan on taking out Al-Hazari as soon as I get the intel about who helped him get the explosives into Oman. I want all the intel I can gather before I kill him. We'll need to run before his men notice."

I was going to ask why she'd have no problem with a SEAL team having her back if she needed but she was pissed my team was in place. There was no doubt the team guys were badass motherfuckers; however, my team ran ten times more ops than they did. As far as experience went, my team was far superior.

Before I could ask, she pointed to a small dirt trail on the left. "We're here. Slow your speed. The checkpoint is around that bend, and the guards will be able to see the dust now that the sun is starting to rise."

I did as she said and pulled off the road, finding a place to ditch the car behind a nice-sized boulder and desert shrub.

Blake knelt down, grabbed a handful of dirt and rubbed it over her face and neck. When she was done dirtying herself, she pulled her knife out and sliced through the sleeves of her long sleeve shirt, using the tip of her blade to lightly scratch marks on her forearm.

I stood, silently watching her, knowing it was essential for her to look like she had been captured but not liking it one bit. This was all wrong. I hated knowing that she had spent years likely doing just this – whatever was needed to survive. More than that, I hated knowing she had the same hash marks on her soul that I had, every kill chipping away at what used to be a complete person. Every life I had ever taken was justified, but that didn't mean late at night when you're left with nothing but your sins you don't remember. There was no box tight enough for the ghosts to be confined.

Even after everything Blake had done to me, I still wanted better for her. It didn't matter how hard I had tried or how many years had passed; I still loved her. I would die loving her.

CHAPTER SIX

Blake

Levi had been silent since we left the car. It was uncomfortable pretending I didn't know him, that he hadn't been the center of my thoughts for over a decade. He was the reason I joined the CIA. I told him a partial truth about being recruited. I was approached, that part was the truth, but I had left out why. I was caught hacking into Alister Bench's files. I had already spent two years gathering information on Alister before the CIA recruited me. I knew all about his dirty dealings. Bench was added to a CIA watchlist when donations he had made went to a charity with known ties to terrorism.

Terrorists and war made for sensational headlines and sold newspapers and advertisements. His media group was thriving in an economy where his competitors were closing up shop. He had found a way to stay ahead of the game. His company had expanded, buying up bankrupt companies and turning them around. He was ten times more powerful now than he was when Levi was a kid. His papers broke all the big stories. Alister Bench was creating news, creating wars, and funding organizations. He was a criminal of the highest order. There was no way to calculate the number of deaths he had on his hands.

Now, the CIA watches him and uses his sloppy interactions with warlords to counteract the plots and find new small organizations to squash before they become too big. That was how we had found Al-Harazi. He was one of Alister's newest pawns. He thought by funding them they would grow in numbers. There was no doubt he knew about the bombing and would have crews on the scene to broadcast live as the horror unfolded. He was in for a rude awakening. The bombing would not happen, and Al-Harazi would be dead.

"There's the village, just over that ridge," I told him.

"Is Al-Harazi there now?" he asked.

"No way to know. If he is following his initial

timeline, yes. He should be getting his convoy ready to go now."

"Perfect. Let's start running. I want him to see us. Draw as much attention as you can. We will head to your tent. Hopefully, he stops us before we make it that far. It will be better if he comes to us. If he doesn't, we will go to him and beg for safe passage," Levi suggested.

"Copy."

I didn't wait for him before I started running at top speed. I wanted to be out of breath and flush by the time we made it to the village; it would only add to the academy award winning performance I was about to pull off. We made it over the ridge, and I allowed myself to slip and fall on my butt, sliding down the small embankment. Levi pulled me up as he passed and we continued. Just as we'd hoped, Al-Hazari was out of his tent loading his caravan. He watched us run into the village, his two guards pointing AK-47s in our direction. It was a wonder the old Russian assault rifles still worked. Al-Hazari was not a wealthy man; his weapons were bottom of the barrel junk no one else wanted.

"Halt," his guard yelled in English.

Levi and I came to a skidding stop in front of the

men. I bent at my waist and held on to my knees, exaggerating my panting.

"I'm sorry, Ahmed. Please excuse the intrusion. I only need to get my belongings so I can go," I wheezed.

I glanced up, and Al-Harazi's eyes widened. "Who did this to you?" he asked.

"I don't know. I was in my bed last night. I was awoken with a hood over my head and taken to the city. I was so scared, Ahmed. They refused to tell me where I was. They wanted to record me for ransom." Tears fell from my eyes, and I hugged my arms around my center. "They said they were going to kill me. I don't mean you any trouble. I only need my bag with my money, so I can leave. I can't be here. If they find me, they'll kill me."

"And this man?" Al-Harazi asked.

"I don't know. He was there. I promised him I had money if he would take me with him."

"Who are you?" Al-Harazi asked Levi.

"Oliver Smith," Levi answered.

"Where did you come from? Why are you here?" Al-Harazi asked.

"Why would I tell you that? So you can hold me for ransom, too? Let this woman get her bag so she can give me the money she promised me." Levi stood up straight and balled his fists, taking a defensive posture.

"You compare me to those savages?" Al-Harazi said and motioned for his men to lower their weapons. "I have never taken a person against their will. I'm here to do God's work."

"That's what the last man said as he stood over me threatening to kill me if my company didn't pay for my return. You'll forgive me if I'm not relying on God to help me out of this situation. I only want the money the woman said she'd give me if I took her with me. I need to leave Yemen, and I need money to bribe someone to take me across the border."

"I'm sorry to hold you up, Ahmed. Thank you for all your hospitality. I'm afraid the men took all of my equipment. I promise you I will still write the story about the good work you are doing. I remember our conversations. I wish you well in your crusade. I'm sorry to run, but I must leave. I don't know if we were followed. I don't want to bring trouble to your door. I owe this man my life, and I must pay him. He managed to escape and took me with him. They were going to kill me." I added some extra tears and shaking for dramatic flair.

Al-Harazi yelled to his men to continue to load the convoy and turned back to us. "Come with me into my tent. You both need medical attention. Tell me what happened."

"Thank you. I would love to clean off my face. Would you spare a drink of water?" I asked.

Al-Harazi and I started walking toward his tent, leaving Levi. "Ma'am, if you wouldn't mind giving me the money so I can leave," he demanded.

"Please, come, we'll clean you up. I promise you safe passage away from this place," Al-Harazi said.

We had him. Levi stood his ground, scanning the area. "Sir, Oliver, you're safe with Ahmed. He is not like those men. He is spreading the word of God, the Bible. Those same men hurt him too. They killed his men and bombed his church."

"Let me clean your wounds, so they don't get infected. If you want to leave after that, I will give you what little money I can spare. We will pray about it," Al-Harazi said.

I wanted to gag at the absurdity of the situation. I wish I could cut his throat right now. This man was disgusting, using the word of God to kill.

"I would appreciate some water and to clean up. Thank you." Levi caught up with us in a few long strides.

We entered Al-Harazi's tent, and it was devoid of all of his personal effects that were once scattered about. He was not planning on returning to the village.

"My apologies. We are moving today. Please stay here; I will fetch supplies."

Al-Harazi left us alone in the tent, and I turned to Levi. "Thank you for saving my life." I started crying again. Knowing we were being listened to, I thought I would continue the show. "I promise I will give you everything I have."

"How do you know these men? Are you sure you're safe? We can run together if you'd like." Levi stopped and dropped his voice lower. "I wish I would've killed all of them."

Al-Harazi reappeared a bucket of water in one hand and two bottles of water in the other. "Here. Clean up." He motioned for me to approach. "How did you escape?" Levi remained quiet and looked around. "No judgment from me. The Bible says an eye for an eye. The ones who took you brutalized you. You have a God-given right to protect yourself and the woman."

"With respect, I wished I could've killed every last one of them." Levi turned to face Al-Harazi. "Maybe I shouldn't be running like a coward. Maybe I should stay and make sure they never try and harm an innocent woman again."

"That would be foolish. You'll come with us. There are many ways to make the men who took you pay. We will talk along the way. If you don't like what I have to say, we'll drop you off, and you buy your way home," Al-Harazi offered.

"Is that what you're doing? Making men like that pay? I'm not interested in praying for these men's souls. I want to send them all to the hell that surely awaits them. I'm a God-fearing man; however, there are times like this I'm too impatient to wait for the wrath of God."

I cleaned my arms with the cloth and bucket of water that Al-Harazi had provided. When I was done, I turned to Levi. "Sir? Would you like me to help you with your face?" I asked.

Levi nodded and walked to me, and I was surprised when he dropped to his knees in front of me and stared up at me with his soulful eyes. They were as unique as I remembered, light gold with a dark ring around the outside. I used to spend hours looking into those eyes; I loved those eyes. None of the pictures I had of us came close to doing the color justice. None of them made me feel the onslaught of emotions that seeing him in person had.

"Miss?" Levi called.

Shit. This was a mission, not a fairytale reunion.

This time when I let the tears stream down my cheeks, they were real. I didn't have to pretend that my heart was broken or I was scared because I was both. "I'm sorry they did this to you. I've never seen anyone get hit so many times." I swiped the tears from my face and picked up the cloth, wringing most of the water back into the bucket before I pressed the soft material to his face. His head leaned into my hand ever so slightly, and I couldn't stop the tears from forming again. Thank God we had an audience, and my tears only added to the authenticity of our cover. I went about wiping down Levi's face and neck as quickly as I could. When I was done, I placed my palm on the side of his face. This very well could be the last time I ever get to touch him again. The first time he left, I didn't get a chance to savor one last touch. I was going to this time. I needed to feel his flesh on mine if after this mission I never saw him again. I would remember the heat under my fingers for the rest of my life.

"I'm sorry," I whispered.

Levi's expression hardened and his golden orbs clouded over with hate I didn't know a human could possess. "They will be too when I find out who they are. Thank you for helping me." Levi quickly stood and backed away from me.

"If it wouldn't be too much trouble, I would like to accept your offer. The woman can keep her money; she'll need it to make her way home as well," Levi said, not trying to mask the anger. Al-Harazi would mistake it for outrage, instead of what it really was – pure unadulterated hatred of me - the woman Levi still believed betrayed him.

CHAPTER SEVEN

Levi

I don't know what made me think I could spend any amount of time with Blake. The moment she looked down at me, I was transported back to a time of peace. When her small, soft hand touched my face, I flashed back to all the times she would run her hand over my stubble. I called it stubble, but I barely needed to shave back then. I was a boy caught up in some nonsensical notion of romance. At her whispered apology, I was ready to forget that she had accepted money from my stepfather to leave me and more than that, she had been negotiating for more. She wasn't happy with the job he had offered, so she waited him out until he started offering the good stuff, paying her way through college, paying off her parents' house. I didn't stick around to see if he offered to buy her one too, but I'm sure he would've.

Those were all of the reasons I had not listened to any of the voicemails she left that day and the months following, nor had I read the text messages, or opened the letters. I was weak when it came to Blake Porter. Now more than ever, I had no business being anywhere near her. I was becoming forgetful in my old age. The pain had dulled to a nagging throb rather than the gaping bleeding wound it had been for so many years. This had to be over soon.

"Yes, that would be fine," Al-Harazi answered.

"What can I do to help? I'd like to earn my keep."

What I really wanted was to get the lay of the land, count how many men he had, and figure out where they would be keeping the weapons for transport.

"That would be most helpful. Come with me. Miss Blake, please rest. We will come and get you when we are ready." I had a sick feeling in my gut when he turned his beady eyes on her. The way he smiled at her was something of a concern as well. He'd planned on taking her if Grayson hadn't gotten to her first. Blake thought she could handle this alone, but I don't think she knew exactly what Al-

Harazi had planned for her. He didn't want her to join in his terror plot; he wanted her – as his woman.

Blake nodded and sat on the only folding chair left in the tent. She was good, that was for sure. The lying, the acting, the agency had turned a perfectly wonderful girl into a conniving con artist. That wasn't entirely true; the day in Alister's office she was well on her way.

I followed Al-Harazi to the convoy. He was greeted by the same two men that flanked Al-Harazi with AKs when we ran up to the camp. I noted the three other men were loading the back of an old pickup.

Al-Harazi spoke to his men in Arabic, his slight British accent disappearing. He was Saudi born and educated in England. Al-Harazi was sent to boarding school in Canterbury from the age of ten to eighteen. After graduation, he stayed in England and attended the University of Cambridge.

I looked at my feet and kicked the small pebbles on the ground while Al-Harazi told his men I was to help load the water jugs into the caravan. As he walked back to his tent, he added for them not to let me out of their sight or around *the woman* without him around. Yes, he wanted Blake for himself.

Well, too fucking bad, he would never get his hands on her.

When the men turned back to me speaking broken English, I pretended not to have understood what Al-Harazi had said as they explained where the water jugs were and how they wanted them in the truck.

Within the hour the trucks were packed, and we were ready to head east to Oman. It was a sixteen-hour drive. Al-Harazi told his men we were to drive straight through and cross the border while it was dark. Once we were in Oman, we would stay the night in a small abandoned military outpost. Blake gave nothing away as Al-Harazi spoke freely in Arabic around us. I wondered if she, too, understood what he was saying as she was pretending to look at the cuts on her arms.

She caught me looking at her and gave me a slight nod before looking back down. Good, she understood as well.

"Miss Blake, you will come with me in the car. It will make for a much more comfortable ride. Oliver, if you wouldn't mind riding in the first truck, there is only one open seat left," Al-Harazi instructed.

Bullshit. There were other seats available, namely in the car with him. He wanted Blake and me separated. Not to mention, the lead vehicle was always the first to take the hit in an ambush.

However, I played along. "Anything you have available is appreciated."

"Very well, let's get moving. We have a day's long drive," he returned.

With one last look at Blake, I followed one of the guards to the front truck. The second guard was already in the driver's seat of Al-Harazi's car. The three other men piled into the second truck. Five men total, all with Russian AK-47s that were so old and battered they were no better than relics that should be mounted on the wall as a showpiece. That was good and bad. Good for me that their guns were more likely to misfire or jam if they tried to get a shot off on me. Bad if we did get ambushed; we were fucked with no weapons in good working order.

I slid into the passenger's seat and immediately went to work on the guard. "Hey, thanks man for letting me come along." I started. "I told my boss that trying to get a manufacturing deal in Yemen was too dangerous. He demanded I come here. It's not his ass that's in danger; you know what I mean?"

"No. I do not know what you are talking about," he answered.

"So, how long is the drive?" I asked.

"Long drive. Sit and be quiet," he demanded, uttering a few words under his breath in Arabic that loosely translated to "pussy American boy."

Perfect. With that out of the way, I sat back and prepared for a long ass drive in a seat that was torn to shreds with the metal springs exposed. My ass was going to be raw by the time we reached the border. Of course, Blake was driving in what would be considered Yemenis luxury. Yet again I get fucked, and Blake makes out like a princess.

Sixteen hours is a long damn time being bounced around in a piece of shit pickup truck with zero shocks. I had been vibrated and shaken half to death. My temper and patience were at polar opposites. My temper was nearing nuclear, and my patience was thin as ice. I hadn't laid eyes on Blake for over sixteen hours. That was a problem, a big one. But I couldn't demand to see her. Each time we had stopped to fill up with gas, I was told to stay in the truck. When I told Mr. I-cannot-drive-worth-a-fuck I needed to take a piss, he walked me to the front of the truck mumbling about filthy Americans urinating in front of a woman. I didn't know what the hell his problem was. It wasn't like I was going to drop trou and pull my dick out for Blake to see, not that she hadn't seen it a hundred times before, or held it and stroked me before she had accepted me into her body. The girl had a mouth on her at eighteen. I couldn't begin to imagine what those soft lips and wicked tongue could do now. That was another issue I had with Blake; she'd ruined me. I compared every blowjob I've received since her to the way Blake sucked me. Life was a cruel bitch. I couldn't enjoy a nice blowjob without visions of Blake invading my thoughts. The first few years after I left her, the bitch infringed on every aspect of my life. I couldn't sleep without dreaming about her. I couldn't have sex without remembering the sweet way she breathed my name as I entered her. The shower reminded me of how she used to like to wash me, her naked soapy body pressing against mine.

She was not the first girl I'd had sex with, nor had she given me my first blowjob, but she was the first and only woman I had ever made love to. She held a lot of firsts for me. Once we had finally broken the seal on having sex, she was wild. She wanted to try everything, and we did. Blake was the first girl I had ever loved, and she was the only one to ever shatter my heart. Blake taught me a lot about love and relationships. Neither were worth it. No good comes from a woman holding so much of you.

"There is the checkpoint. You shut your mouth," the guard told me.

Al-Harazi's car passed and pulled in front of us to the barricade. Within a matter of minutes, money was exchanged, and we were waved through.

Now that Al-Harazi's car was in the lead, I strained in the darkness to catch a glimpse of the back seat. I only saw the silhouette of one figure. The thought that Blake's head may very well be laying in his lap ratcheted up my anger. He would die a painful, drawn-out death if he'd touched her.

The cars came to a stop, and the back door of Al-Harazi's car came open. He stepped out, Blake cradled in his arms. As I exited the truck, I thought of all the ways I was going to torture him. Blake was unmoving; her head rested on his chest, her right arm fell out to the side. Her fingers twitched, and she gave me the sign for *all good*. She might've thought *she* was all good; however, I was not.

Her next signal came quick, two hours then the go sign. I had to admit Blake was a great field agent, cool under pressure and smart. Her signals had been clear and concise. Her time frame was perfect. The faster she killed him, the sooner we could continue to Muscat. We'd have another six-hour drive to our evac point.

"We are going to retire for the evening. We will leave at sunrise for the rest of our journey. Mr. Oliver, there are many places we can drop you along the way. However, if you wish, I can deliver you safely to the embassy. Miss Blake has told me she owes you a debt of gratitude for saving her life. I feel as though I owe you as well," Al-Harazi told me, holding Blake close to his body as if he was staking claim to the woman.

In his dreams.

"The embassy would be appreciated if it is not out of your way," I responded.

"Very well."

Al-Harazi inclined his head in acknowledgment and turned to his guard, telling him not to let me out of his sight and to shoot me if I tried to leave.

So much for hospitality.

CHAPTER EIGHT

Blake

I was going to vomit if Al-Harazi petted me like a dog one more time. For sixteen hours I had to sit in the backseat with the filthy pig as he tried to soothe me. All the while I had to play the part of the scared little girl as I planned how I was going to kill him.

This was the first time that he had overtly touched me in any fashion. In the past, I had caught him staring at me, and he had made references to us leaving together to spread the good word in the other countries that needed it; however, he'd never elaborated on where or in what capacity my presence would be.

Al-Harazi had been speaking to his men, ordering his guards to watch Levi. I hoped that Levi caught my hand gestures. It wasn't like I could open my eyes to verify. I was supposed to be asleep curled up in Al-Harazi's arms, appreciating the protection he'd offered. When he'd started telling the driver that we could stop at any time to *dump the American,* I waited an appropriate amount of time before I started crying. When Al-Harazi asked me what was wrong, I told him how the man had saved my life, how Oliver Smith had found a way to escape and instead of leaving me there, he took me with him. I hoped that if I told him how indebted I was to Levi, he wouldn't leave him somewhere. I was counting on the fact Al-Harazi thought that he was going to keep me as his woman. He wouldn't want to upset me and have me try and flee. Keeping me happy meant he could control me.

The door to a room creaked, and I continued to feign sleep. When I was lowered onto a bed, and my hair was brushed off my face, it was then I opened my eyes.

"Where are we?" I whispered.

"We have crossed into Oman. Sleep. We will leave again soon," he answered.

The bed was a small twin-sized military style cot; which made sense. We were at an outpost of some sort.

"Where will you be staying?" I asked.

"With the men, of course."

Game time.

"What? You can't leave me here. Someone can take me again." I pretended to panic and scrambled to get to my feet.

"It would be highly inappropriate for me to sleep in a room with a woman that is not my wife." He sounded affronted.

But I suppose the prostitutes I had watched exit his tent night after night were deemed appropriate because there was no sleeping involved.

"I'm sorry, I don't mean to offend you. I'm just so scared. May I please sleep in the car? At least the doors lock. I can't sleep by myself."

I needed him in the room with me. Sneaking into a barrack with five tangos and one friendly was not impossible, but it would make my exit difficult. Even though I didn't have the intel I wanted, I had to take Al-Harazi out now. There wouldn't be another opportunity and this plan had the added benefit of stranding his men in the middle of the desert.

"You will not sleep in the car like a vagabond." Al-Harazi's gaze was appraising as he looked around the room. There was no other bed except the small cot. The look on his face told me he was about to tell me no. I had to change tactics.

"You can have the bed in here. I will sleep on a bedroll on the floor. Please, I am begging you."

"Very well. Let me tell Amir to bring you a blanket," he relented.

When Al-Harazi left the room and I patted my pocket, I had my knife but still needed a backup plan. There was nothing in here if he took my knife. I would only have my hands. I prayed we were far enough away from the men that they wouldn't hear the struggle.

"Here you are," Al-Harazi said as he entered the room.

"Thank you. You're too kind. I won't be any trouble." I took the blankets and quickly made myself a bed on the floor and laid down.

"Sleep well, Miss Blake," Al-Harazi said when he sat on the edge of the cot, slipping his sandals off his feet leaving the rest of his clothes on.

I closed my eyes and waited. I heard the guard pass by the door; however, he never entered. Al-Harazi's breathing had evened out and loud snoring started. I had told Levi two hours to go; with no watch this was going to be a best-guess scenario. The guard had walked by the door three times; experience told me that more than likely they patrolled in thirty-minute rotations. I had roughly ten minutes until the next pass.

I slipped my knife out of my pocket and flipped the blade open. Feeling the knurled metal of the handle made me feel safer, more in control of my surroundings. On silent feet, I made my way to Al-Harazi's bedside. Without warning or fanfare, I slit Al-Harazi's throat from ear to ear. It was quick, it was precise, and it was fatal. I used his headscarf to wipe the blood off my hands and knife and tried to position it to conceal the wound, hoping to buy us a few extra minutes before his men saw he was dead.

Before I could move the door came open and Amir, Al-Harazi's right-hand man, walked in.

"What are you doing?" he demanded.

Amir's weapon was up and trained on me. From this distance, I had no chance of disarming him. I had to talk my way out of this.

"I got scared. I was going to wake Ahmed," I answered.

Amir took a step toward me, close enough that if he looked, he would see the now blood-soaked scarf. There was movement behind Amir, and before he could take another step, hands came up from behind him, one to his forehead and one to his chin. In a fast jerk, his neck snapped and Levi lowered him to the ground.

Thank God.

Levi gestured for me to be silent and removed the AK from Amir's lifeless body, motioning me to follow him. Four men remained. Hopefully, they were all sleeping and we could get a head start before they woke up and started shooting at us. That was another suck-ass part of the job – being shot at.

"Did you grab the keys to the trucks?" I whispered.

"No need."

"Listen speed-racer; they will know the roads better than us. If you think you can outrun them, you can't," I explained.

"I said, no need," he growled.

Well someone was an ass when he was tired. I wanted to question him further but thought better of it. We had six hours in a car together, and the last thing I wanted was to start a pissing match before the drive.

Levi led us to the car. I rounded the truck and glanced in the backseat. There were at least ten AKs in the back and water jugs that had not been there when I exited the car.

"Get in," Levi demanded when he saw me gawking at the stash.

I did as I was told and remained quiet as he pulled away from the outpost.

"You still have your phone?" he asked.

"I do," I answered, not offering the phone I knew he wanted.

"May I have it?" he clipped.

"Not until you tell me what is going on, and what *no need* means exactly."

If he thought he was going to growl at me and push me around, he had another thing coming. I might not have been special ops, but I was a damn good field agent. If he wouldn't extend me the courtesy of respect as a colleague, I would demand it.

"Listen, Blake..."

"No way. You listen. You will extend the same consideration to me you would a fellow teammate. Whether we like it or not, we're partners on this op. And might I remind you, you're the one that demanded you accompany me."

"And it's a damn good thing I did, or you'd be dead right now. What did you think was going to happen back there?" he scolded.

The nerve of this asshole.

"I was going to talk my way closer to him then I

was going to kill him. I've been in tighter situations than that. I didn't need you to come in and save the day."

"No need means that the rest of the men are dead," he explained. "I need the phone."

I was impressed he had taken out four men on his own, not that I would tell him that. And as much as I'd love to know how he did it, I wouldn't give him the satisfaction of asking.

"Here." I pulled the old-school flip phone out of the pocket of my cargo pants and held it out. "Do you want me to dial a number for you?"

Levi quickly rattled off a number for me to dial and I pushed send and handed the phone to him.

After a moment of silence, he said, "Dragonfly. Pink. Niner Zulu seven two five."

He told whoever had answered the operation code name, the color of the day, and his personal call in number to verify his identity. "Mission complete. Six tangos down and the package is secure en route to Evac One." After another pause, he continued. "Affirmative. Patch me through."

I wished he would've put the call on speaker so I could've heard the other end of the conversation. I hated that I was left in the dark. I took a minute to look at Levi, really look at the man he had become. It was hard to make out his features in the dark, but I had those memorized. I was more interested in the way he now carried himself, how he'd grown from a teenage football star to a hardened warrior. The old Levi was kind and considerate. He was so full of life that everyone gravitated toward him. I was sure some of it had to do with how good looking he was, but it was more than that. He was charismatic and friendly. This new Levi was closed off and cold. Maybe it was just me he was like this with. Even after all these years, he still thought that I had betrayed him. My heart broke at the thought of him walking around all these years hating me.

"Copy that," he said and shut the phone.

I waited, and when he didn't relay any information I broke down and asked, "Everything good?"

"Yes," he answered.

"You're gonna play it this way? Not give me any information?"

With a sigh, he said, "Jasper and Lenox made it to Muscat. Al-Harazi had a three-man crew there to rig each embassy. They were disguised as government workers checking the power grid. They had all the right credentials. Grayson and Clark are checking into who forged their documents or if they had backing from the government."

"They didn't have help from the Omani government," I said.

"How do you know that? They have more financial backing than we originally thought."

Damn. I didn't know how much to tell him. On one hand, he needed the intel, on the other, it would make me look like I was exactly what he thought I was – a traitor; that I had more to do with Alister Bench than I did.

"They have an American investor. Someone who funnels money to them for his own personal gain," I explained.

"An American? Who? How do you know?" he asked.

I guess it was time to tell him the truth. It wasn't like he could hate me more than he did.

"Alister Bench."

CHAPTER NINE

Levi

She said my stepfather's name and I almost veered off the small dirt path we were on.

"I see. So, you're still in contact with the old man?" My lips curled in disgust. "How does your boss feel about you being in bed with a man that funds terrorists? Or are you keeping that a secret from him too?"

She had a lot of nerve saying that man's name to me. My thoughts briefly flashed to my mom and sister. I wondered if they knew that Mr. Moneybucks was a criminal. I doubted they even cared as long as he kept the bank account full and they could spend all they wanted. It seemed like all the women I'd once loved were nothing more than money hungry bitches.

"I haven't seen that man in twelve years."

"And was that the time I caught the two of you conspiring? Tell me, were you helping him fund terrorists then too?"

"You're a dick. Do you even listen to yourself when you talk? If I was conspiring with him would I be telling you he was the one channeling money to Al-Harazi?"

She was right. Rationally I knew she wasn't helping Bench. However, there was no part of me that was rational when it came to Blake Porter.

"Did you listen to any of the voicemails from that day?" she asked. Her voice had softened, and my heart clenched. She sounded so much like the Blake I loved, sweet and gentle.

"Why does that matter?" I didn't want to talk about that day. I couldn't take anymore lies. "You know, I should be thanking you. It is because of that day, what you did to me, that I am the man I am. You killed a part of me, the young pussy-whipped idiot. That boy never would've made it through selection. You taught me a valuable lesson. A lesson that has kept me alive."

"It didn't have to be this way," she whispered.

"No? What other way did you think this was gonna play out? Did you think Alister was gonna give you all that money and you were gonna keep fucking me? No thanks, honey. You were good, but I don't fuck Alister's whores."

The instant the words came out of my mouth I wished I could draw them back in. As pissed as I was at her, this was not me. I was never cruel just to be hurtful.

I was about to apologize when she changed the subject. "The CIA recruited me when they caught me hacking into Alister's financials. He had been on their watch list, and they wanted the information I had gathered on him. At the time, I had every intention of finishing school and being a reporter. I wanted to expose Alister, but the agency got to me first. They left me no choice; I either worked for them, or I was facing federal jail time. Obviously, I accepted their offer. I was assigned to a special task force to take down high-powered American players that funded terror organizations overseas." Blake stopped and took a deep breath before she continued. "What you thought you saw that day wasn't me betraying you. And after you left and I realized I had lost you forever, I made it my mission to take down Alister Bench. It is only now I have the evidence I need to destroy him. Everything up until this point has been circumstantial at best. Over the years we've allowed him to get comfortable. It's paid off, and now he is complacent and thinks he has outsmarted the government. He no longer goes to great lengths to hide his dealings. He's lazy, and I have everything I need to bury him."

There was a lot of information there to sift through, but something was nagging at me. "If my stepfather has ties to terrorism, why have I never been questioned? I have a top-secret clearance. The government crawls up my ass investigating every aspect of my life."

"Because I cleared you. I knew you knew nothing about Alister's dealings. And truthfully, the director agreed that keeping you in the dark was best. The fewer people that knew, the less of a chance Alister would get tipped off."

I didn't know what to say about that, so I opted to remain quiet. Blake seemed to be lost in her thoughts as well. I wasn't sure if I should be grateful that she had cleared my name with the director or pissed that I wasn't trusted enough to be told. What other secrets did she know about my family that she wasn't telling me? Did my mother know? Was my sister involved? She worked for Alister at one of his newspapers. I wanted to know what had motivated Alister to fund terror organizations and I wondered if that was the reason he was so against me joining the military. My mom wasn't happy about the idea but only because she thought I could play professional football and I would be able to support her. She didn't have any real objections until Alister flat out refused to entertain the idea of me joining the Army.

We drove in silence for a long while; I kept replaying what Blake had said over and over. *It didn't have to be this way.* What the hell had she meant by that? I popped off at the mouth with something ridiculous to hurt her; however, I couldn't begin to imagine what other way she thought things could go.

What you thought you saw that day wasn't me betraying you. I saw her with my own two eyes negotiating with Alister about the amount of money it would take to have her convince me not to leave for the Army. I heard the girl I loved put a price tag on our relationship and agree to break up with me.

Alister had hated her and her family. He thought they were beneath him because they were good, hardworking middle-class people. I needed to get back to Georgia so I could dig into what my family had been doing since I'd left. Blake could go back to

DC or wherever she lived and go about living her life. It was very doubtful we would cross paths again.

"There is a hotel up ahead. We're gonna stop for a few hours and wait for Clark and Grayson to catch up. Jasper and Lenox will come by and pick us up."

I had meant to tell her earlier there was a change in the EXFIL plan but I was derailed by talks of Alister.

"Okay," she agreed, her voice devoid of any emotion.

I knew I should've apologized for my earlier outburst, but I wouldn't. Some things are best left water under the bridge. Our shared history was one of those things.

When we pulled into the hotel, Blake had crawled in the backseat and put the weapons on the floorboards, using her legs to try and conceal most of them. Not that it was unusual in this part of the world to see guns, but we didn't want to advertise we had them.

I quietly exited the car and went about getting us a room. I contemplated getting two; she had proven she could take care of herself. Despite what I had told her about saving her ass when Amir found her, I was sure she would've gotten herself out of the situation. If I was honest with myself, it was kind of hot the way she'd handled Al-Harazi and how calm she remained when she watched me take down Amir.

I opted for one room, tactically it was the smart move, and there was the added benefit of Blake likely being pissed. By the time I had walked back to the car, Blake had already jimmied the backseat down and secured all but two of the AKs I had taken from Al-Harazi's men. I pulled the car around to the backside of the hotel where our room was located, and we quickly made our way into the room.

"You mind if I wash up first?" she asked.

"No, go ahead."

That would give me time to think about how I was going to play this. We had at least three hours until Clark and Grayson caught up with us and possibly a few hours after that depending on what Jasper and Lenox had come up with to get us the fuck out of this country. Lenox said the commander was calling in a marker with a friend who owned a resort in Salalah. The man owned a private jet that could fly us out of Oman without the normal documentation.

I doubled checked the door was locked and kept the blinds drawn. The room was decent by in-the-middle-of-nowhere standards. It was a typical low-cost motel in Oman. Cream walls, ceramic tile floor, a bed, a chair, and a bathroom. The bathroom was an open space with a toilet and a spigot on the wall; there was no bathtub or shower stall. I heard the water turn on and had to grab on to the arm of the chair when I thought about Blake in the other room showering.

I could remember every inch of her soft flesh. Once upon a time, it had belonged to me. I'd kissed and licked every part of her. The water continued to run in the bathroom, and with it, my imagination ran wild. I wondered if she still liked to be kissed while she orgasmed. My dick hardened at the memory of her above me, riding me, leaning over me to take my mouth as she started to come. How many times over the years had I tortured myself and jerked off to the memory of her? Too many to count.

The sound of automatic gunfire pulled me from my memory. I grabbed one of the AKs off the bed and gently pulled back the curtain. There were a few buildings around us but mostly wide open barren desert. The gunshots rang out again, and a pickup with two men in the bed of the truck drove by, both with rifles in their hands shooting into the sand.

"We good?" I heard from behind me, the water still running in the bathroom.

I looked over my shoulder, and Blake was

standing in the doorway of the bathroom buttoning her cargo pants. Before she had them fully fastened I caught a glimpse of purple panties. My eyes roamed to her flat stomach that showed signs of a six pack, then up further to a purple bra. Her full breasts spilled over the cups, giving me just a hint of nipple. The girl's body I could clearly remember had changed. The swell of her soft belly was now hardened muscle, her once perky breasts seemed to have gotten bigger. I wish I could've asked her to turn around because I would bet her ass was perfection. She had the body of an athlete.

"Levi," she snapped.

"Five by five."

She nodded her head and turned back toward the bathroom giving me a view of her scarred back. It looked like she had been whipped or sliced. Five long red scars crisscrossed her back.

"Stop staring, it's not polite," she said as she slammed the door.

Holy shit. Where the hell had Blake been over the last eight years?

CHAPTER TEN

Blake

The last twenty-four hours had caught up with me. I was mentally wrecked. After two failed attempts to pull my damn shirt over my head, I finally had it on and was preparing myself to face Levi. We were almost done. Just a few more hours and the rest of the team would be here, and I could go home. I had days' worth of reports to write, and I welcomed the distraction. Seeing Levi again had fucked with my head in ways I could never imagine.

How was it possible that my heart still wanted a man that hated me and called me a whore? He had no respect for me as an operator nor as a person, yet I couldn't stop myself from wanting to fall into his arms. I was stupid and living in some fantasyland where I would prove to him once and for all that I had not deceived him, and we could wipe the last twelve years clean. Even if I could, he wasn't the same boy I fell in love with, and I wasn't the young naïve girl. I was the lead agent on a special task force to take down INCONUS players that funded terrorists. He was a special operator with a black ops team that, as far as the intelligence community knew, didn't exist. We both had new lives, and those lives didn't include the other person.

There was a knock at the door followed by, "Are you okay?"

Shit, how long had I been hiding in here?

"I'm good," I answered and opened the door, coming face to face with Levi.

His eyes freely roamed over my now dressed body, and I wanted to shrink under his scrutiny. I had lost my womanly figure years ago. The more hours I trained, the harder and more toned my body became. I had lost all the soft curves men tend to like. Between my boyish frame and all the scars, I was nothing to look at.

Levi's hand came up to my face; his thumb gently rubbed the apple of my cheek. It had been so long since I had felt his hands on me. I leaned into his touch, and his thumb stilled before he started to pull it away. My hand came up and covered his, not allowing him to retreat. I needed this, needed the connection. It had been a shit two days and years since I'd had any human contact.

"Don't mistake this for something it's not," he warned.

"I won't," I answered.

Our eyes locked, his pupils dilated, and his mouth got tight.

"Just because my dick is stupid and wants you doesn't mean I've forgotten."

His words were harsh, but his touch was not. His large hand gently cradled my face as his thumb moved again, grazing my soft skin.

"I understand." And I did. I knew what this was. Two people giving in to their attraction, using each other to burn off the adrenaline of a mission. It was nothing more.

"I hope you do."

Those were the last words he spoke before my back was pushed up against the wall and his lips were on my neck. They were not gentle and sensual; they were needy and demanding.

Levi's mouth didn't leave my neck as his hands went to my ass and he hoisted me into his arms, forcing me to wrap my legs around him. I was tossed on the bed, and my clothes were torn from my body in a mad rush, leaving me nude on the cool bedcover. I watched with rapt attention as he pulled his shirt over his head. Muscle over muscle – that was the only way to describe his chest and tight abs. It was a far cry from the boyish six-pack he once had. His pants and boxers came down at the same time, leaving his erection on full display. My mouth watered at the thought of taking him past my lips and down my throat. Back in the day, I had mastered how to make him squirm. I knew he loved it when I tongued the thick vein on the underside of his dick. It drove him crazy when I scraped my teeth on his engorged head. I could make him beg me to let him finish after I'd spent a good amount of time teasing him and working him up. I used to love to suck him off; loved the feel of him in my mouth and the power I had when he was at my mercy.

His knee came to the bed, forcing me to spread my legs further, and his mood shifted as his large frame loomed over me. "I don't have protection," he said, regret evident in his voice.

This had not been very well thought out. We were in the middle of a mission, not a date. Of course, he wouldn't be carrying a condom in his pocket.

"I have an IUD, and it's been five years for me. I'm clean," I told him.

His eyes flared, and there was a quick in draw of breath. "You sure? It hasn't been that long for me, but I'm always careful."

"I trust you," I whispered, and I did, even though I knew he'd never trust me again.

He settled himself into the cradle of my legs, and in one long hard thrust, he pushed inside of me. It was both the best feeling in the world and the worst. He set a bruising pace, fucking me with a force he never had before. This was a first for us; the first time we had had sex without a barrier between us and the first time he had fucked me. There was no mistaking that was what it was, and he fucked me senseless. I matched his powerful thrusts and bucked up to meet him, chasing the orgasm that was just below the surface. He drove into me over and over, never once kissing me, not whispering the sweet words he used to in my ear as he made love to me.

He lifted his chest off mine, settling back on his knees. He hitched my legs over his shoulders before leaning down again, almost bending me double. The new angle was deep, and I had no way to stop the onslaught of a pleasure. His pelvis ground down on my clit at the same time he tongued my nipple. The problem was, he knew me. He knew all the ways to catch my body on fire and leave me hanging on the edge. I was so close. He knew what I needed and wasn't going to give it to me. He loved to hear me beg.

"You want it, baby?" he asked.

My body locked tight, and my heart squeezed. It had been twelve long, excruciating years since I had heard those words. I felt my eyes prick with tears and turned my head to the side, not wanting to look at him. My body needed this; it craved the release. But my heart knew better.

I nodded my answer hoping he would hurry and give me what I desperately wanted.

"You know better. I want the words, Blake. You're so close," he said as he continued to give me short jabs, keeping me on the edge.

"Please," I begged, breaking down. I couldn't take it. I didn't want to hear him talk. I wanted my orgasm and nothing more.

"There it is," he rasped. "Goddamn, you're sexy as hell with your tits bouncing each time I shove my dick into your warm wet cunt."

"Oh my God," I screamed out. So close. I never thought I would like dirty talk during sex. I had never heard it before. And as much as I hated the word cunt, right then, while his dick was inside of me, it sounded deliciously filthy.

"I'm there, Blake. Come with me." His mouth was back on my nipple, and he let loose.

I couldn't hold back; my orgasm broke, leaving me breathless. A few moments later Levi followed and let go inside of me.

We remained still while our breathing came under control. His head rested on my chest. His breath was coming out in pants, the warm air teasing my nipple. The connection had not been severed; his hard dick was still planted deep. I didn't move a muscle while I savored the last moments of our joining. Undoubtedly this would be the last time I would ever have Levi. I would think about the ramifications of what that meant later. When I was alone, and I could cry for everything that was stolen from us. We had been destined for a beautiful life. That was gone now. All that was left was regret and one last fuck before he said goodbye again, not that he said it the first time he left.

Levi pulled out and rolled to the side. Getting off the bed he went to the bathroom, giving me a perfect view of his tight ass and back. He had a large tattoo across his shoulder blades. It read – *So Others May Live*. That was the reason he joined the Army, to fight for and protect the ones that couldn't. He would risk his life so others wouldn't have to.

I was still thinking about his tattoo when he came back to the bed with a towel in his hand. He sat on the bed and moved to wipe between my legs when I stopped him.

"I can do that," I told him with a little more attitude than I had intended. It was one thing to give him my body but this... this was intimate, a lover's work to clean and care for their partner.

We weren't lovers. We were two people who had fucked. That was all.

CHAPTER ELEVEN

Levi

I had screwed up in so many ways I couldn't figure out where to begin to mentally chastise myself. I had no business touching Blake, yet I did. Not only had I touched her, but I also fucked her. I treated her like she was nothing more than a warm body to abuse. I had never, not once in the all the times we were together, fucked her. It didn't matter the pace, the position, or the location – I had always made love to her. Even if I had her bent over the hood of my truck for a quickie, I still whispered how beautiful she was, how much I loved and adored her, how much the gift of her body meant to me.

I was a dick.

"I know you can. But I want to." It was wrong

of me to demand this of her. I was taking more from her than I deserved, using this small gesture to assuage some of my guilt for basically ripping off her clothes and taking her. I made sure she was taken care of physically, and there was no mistaking that she had gotten what she needed, but emotionally, I gave her nothing. Not even a kiss. I ached to feel her lips on mine; that was exactly why I held back.

She was stiff and uncomfortable as I cleaned between her legs, wiping the evidence of our shared release away. To make matters worse, we didn't use a condom. Never had I gone bareback; not in a drunken one-night stand, not in the height of passion – never.

"Fuck. I'm sorry Blake," I said.

"For?" she asked, her brow pulling together.

"I shouldn't have done that. Everything is hard enough. I shouldn't have lost control and touched you," I admitted.

"You mean you shouldn't have fucked me?" she questioned.

I cringed at her using such a crass word to describe us having sex. "Yes."

"Why are you sorry? I'm not. I think we both needed it, the rush of the op, the thrill of the kill. I know I needed a way to burn off all of the adrenaline. Was it not good for you?"

I'd give her props for trying; however, no amount of CIA training could hide the truth in her eyes. I also knew Blake straight down to her soul. She hadn't had sex in five years, confirming what I already knew- Blake didn't give her body easily. She could play like she was unaffected that I'd used her, but she was hurt. I debated on calling her out on her bullshit but decided that would make me an even bigger dick to make her admit that she was hurt. Instead, I decided to play along and let it go while imparting a little truth.

"The sex was always good between us, best I'd ever had. If you're good, I am, too. As long as we both understand what that was."

"I understand just fine, Levi. I'm not some stupid eighteen-year-old girl with stars in her eyes. Thanks for the fuck. I'm gonna go clean up."

Well, that didn't go as well as I'd hoped. She got up and strutted her fine ass to the bathroom and slammed the door, leaving me sitting on the bed with my dick still hard. I was honest with Blake when I told her the sex was always good with her. Sex was never the issue, just like now, my dick was always ready to go multiple rounds. I couldn't get enough of her; she was made to take me. She was mine in every way, that was until her and Alister Bench had fucked everything up.

I found my clothes and got dressed as she was walking back into the room, a small towel wrapped around her body. She snatched her clothes off the floor and dropped the towel.

"What?" she asked when she caught me staring at her.

"What are you doing?" I asked.

Now the woman was taunting me on purpose. She could've dressed in the bathroom or asked me to turn my back, but instead, she made sure I had a full view of her sexy little body.

"I'm getting dressed. Does it offend you that I'm naked?" Her hand went to her naked hip as she cocked her head to the side. "When did you become such a prude?"

Oh hell no.

"A prude? Baby, why don't you step a little closer and I'll show you just how much of a prude I am not." She dropped her hand and started to move. "Before you take another step I'm gonna warn you, if you come to me, I'm gonna bend you over that bed and fuck you so hard and good you'll feel me for a week. I'm not playing with you, Blake."

She flashed a cocky grin and stepped closer. "Is that so? What's to say you won't be the one feeling me for a week. You think I can't handle big bad Levi McCoy fucking me?" She made a tsking noise and continued. "Have you forgotten how much I used to love when you bent me over and tugged my hair?"

I had already pulled my shirt back off, and my pants and boxers were in the process of falling to the floor.

"This is gonna be rough, baby," I warned.

"I hoped it would be," she sassed and took the last step, stopping in front of me.

I had her bent over the bed, and my dick lined up before she could register what was happening. She wanted this rough and dirty; I'd gladly oblige.

In this position, I could see there were more scars across her back than I had originally thought. Pushing the thoughts of how she got those out of my head, I folded over her, placing my mouth at her ear.

"There is not a goddamn thing I don't remember about you," I growled and pushed inside of her. Gathering a handful of her silky strands, I pulled hard, making sure she knew just how true my words were. "You love it when I pull your hair. You like it when I'm driving my dick deep inside of you. But you love it even more when you're on your knees in front of me, and I tug it as I'm feeding you my dick. Do you remember that Blake? How much you loved to suck my dick?"

"Yes," she screamed, and I quickened my pace.

There was no way to describe the sensation of being inside of Blake again. There were so many emotions wrapped up in my feelings toward her. Anger and hate mixed together with love and lust. It was explosive and rough. I pounded into her remembering how she ripped my heart out.

"I did forget one thing – how fucking good you feel. The memory was never this good."

"Yes," she repeated.

"You're gonna beg me to let you come," I demanded, the bed frame scraping on the tile floor as I slammed into her.

"I'm ready, Levi," she said, panting and pushing her ass back in perfect rhythm.

"Is that how you ask?" I asked, and brought my hand down to her ass, the sound of the slap echoing in the room. "I didn't forget that either, baby. In all these years have you found someone new to smack your ass the way you need it?"

"Fuck you," she spat out and shoved her hips back. "Lie down, I want on top," she demanded.

When I didn't do as she demanded, she twisted

her hips and dislodged my dick. Scrambling on the bed, she left me standing there, my dick throbbing, dripping with her wetness.

"Lie down, Levi. I'm done fucking around."

This was new; she had never been demanding during sex before. It was sexy as hell. I did her bidding and laid down. She quickly threw her leg over me and fisted my dick, her small hand gliding easily from root to tip. She lined us up and slammed down. This was going to be too much. She went to work riding my dick hard and fast.

"Is this how you like it?" she asked as she swiveled her hips each time she bottomed out. "I seem to remember you loved it when I was on top. You said you liked to watch my tits sway. Tell me, Levi, is the view as good as you remembered?"

Yeah, she was pissed, and it was totally hot. I let my hands roam. Starting at her thighs, I moved my way over her flat stomach up to her breasts and cupped them both. They were more than a handful, with perfect raspberry colored nipples that were hard and begging for attention.

"Better than I remembered. Lean down so I can taste your…" I almost said mouth. Fuck. We couldn't go there. I had to keep that barrier up for both of us. I was afraid the moment I felt her soft lips on mine it would be game over. "...pretty tits. I want to suck on them while you ride me."

She leaned forward, balancing herself on one elbow while her other hand went to my hair. The touch was soft and intimate. She gently ran her fingers through my short hair, making years of memories wash over me. Not the sexual recollections that I could handle; the memories of loving tender moments between us were threatening to shatter what was left of my soul.

I lifted my head and took her nipple into my mouth, so damn sweet. I tightened my grip on her hips and rocked her harder. I needed to concentrate on fucking her before I did something stupid like forgive her and beg her not to leave.

"Levi," she moaned.

That was better, that was what I needed. "Right here, Blake. You close?" I asked, knowing damn well she was.

"So close. Help me."

I pushed up, held her tight, and helped her as she rode my dick in a frenzied race to completion. I felt when she let go, and I followed, once again spilling myself into her. With nothing between us, the sensation was magnified times a hundred. I could feel every twitch of her pussy as she climaxed.

She gave me her weight, and I wrapped my arms around her, holding her to me. Having her in my arms again made me ache inside for all that I had lost. I would give this one gift to myself knowing that I would pay for it later. While I was alone in my bed at night, I would think back to this moment with Blake soft and sated in my arms, and it would hurt like a bitch. Even knowing all of that, I couldn't bear the thought of losing her heat.

One last time I would hold the woman I loved close to my heart.

CHAPTER TWELVE

Blake

After round two I cleaned up again, this time dressing in the bathroom. I thought better of taunting Levi a third time, though he could've gone again if his still-hard dick was any indication. He was right. I would definitely feel him for a week – not that I minded. I liked knowing that after I went home to my lonely apartment in Virginia, I would remember he had been inside of me.

Levi and I didn't talk about what had happened between us. It wasn't awkward, but it wasn't comfortable either. I suspected it had less to do with the sex and more to do with our past. It was a huge elephant in the room. I wished he would've asked me about that day, but he stubbornly avoided it, and I was done begging him. I did it for months after he left and again today when I asked him if he'd listened to the voicemails I had left him. He had made his choice. Even if I knew he didn't understand what had really happened that day and I'd done nothing wrong, I couldn't *make* him do anything he didn't want to do. And he was hell-bent on hating me.

When Clark and Grayson showed up, the room seemed to close in on me. It was obvious how close Levi was to his teammate. Clark may not have known the details of our past, but he certainly blamed me for any perceived pain I may have caused Levi. Clark had been watching me with the eye of a well-trained operator over the last hour as we waited for Jasper and Lenox to meet us so we could head to the airport. The airplane was fueled and waiting on the tarmac for us. I couldn't wait to go home and get away from these men.

I caught Clark staring at me again, and I snapped. "Do you have a problem with me?"

I turned to fully face Clark, who was sitting in the only chair available in the room. Levi had stretched out on the bed and was reading something on a tablet that Grayson had provided.

"No problem with you," he answered, uncaring I had called him out.

"What's the problem then? Why do you keep looking at me like I'm a hostile that you're guarding?"

"Because I haven't figured out if you are yet," he returned.

My eyes narrowed, and he remained cool under my stare. "Come again? You think I'm a hostile?"

"I'm not sure what you are. But I'd say there is more to you than you want me to know."

"You'd be right. I don't want you to know anything about me. After today you'll never see me again. There's no need for you to know a goddamn thing about me."

The fucking nerve of this man. I was none of his business.

"How'd you kill Al-Harazi?" he asked.

"I sliced his throat and ended his vile existence. Would you like to examine my blade?" I pulled my Benchmade knife out of my pocket and with a flick of my thumb I released the three-and-a-half-inch blade and held it out for Clark to see.

What the hell was he accusing me of?

"I know he's dead. We stopped to clean up the bodies. I checked your work; it was clean and precise. No hesitation marks."

"And? That's a problem for you?" I asked.

"Normally no. It's damn impressive. I know only

a handful of men that are comfortable with that kind of kill and most still leave hesitation marks."

"So, because I'm not a man, you're questioning me?"

"No. I'm trying to figure out if you're a complete psychopath with no empathy for human life or if you're so good at your job you've learned how to shut off that portion of your brain while you're executing a kill order. Then, of course, there is the option that you learned that particular skill as a coping mechanism, a learned behavior to completely turn off your emotions as a way to protect yourself."

Well damn, now he was getting a little too close to the truth. I was damn good at my job. He had the events out of order, but he was getting close. I had used what I learned as a CIA agent to my advantage and found I could shut my emotions down and not feel the crushing weight of loss.

"When you figure it out you'll have to let me know. In the meantime, all you need to know is I'm a damn good agent, and over the years I've learned how to execute any order I'm given. I'm the senior field agent in my unit, and I have earned the respect of the agency. But I'm sure you know that, seeing as you've had hours to dig through my life. Like I said, you don't have to worry about me. In a few more hours this will all be over, and you'll never see me again."

"That's doubtful," he muttered under his breath.

I looked at Grayson, the man who had started this shitstorm, and contemplated kicking his ass. He sat on the edge of the bed looking at the floor, pretending he hadn't heard mine and Clark's exchange. Levi was still sprawled out on the bed; he, however, was looking directly at me. Fuck him, too. If he didn't like the way I was talking to his teammate, he could suck it.

FIVE LONG, tedious hours later we were at the airfield. Levi had done a pre-flight walk-through with the pilot, Grayson, Jasper, and Lenox were already on the plane. I wasn't ready to be stuck in close quarters with the men yet. Instead, I opted to wait on the tarmac. It was hot as blazes outside; the slight wind feeling like a hair dryer blowing hot air in your face. There was a row of small hangars that provided enough cover that the desert sand wasn't blowing on us as well. Levi announced we were ready to go and turned to walk up the steps to the jet when a glint caught my eye.

"Sniper!" I yelled, and instinctively threw my body over Levi's back, taking us both to the ground.

Hot searing pain burned through my shoulder as I rolled off Levi to draw my sidearm. Clark had already begun to return fire. Levi regained his footing, and he, too, was throwing bullets. I took cover behind the car and took a moment to slow my breathing. I saw the flash of a scope again and scanned the area for any other shooters.

"One shooter, twelve o'clock," I yelled out.

"Copy," Levi returned. We were at a disadvantage being out in the open. There was no point in me shooting my .45 at more than four hundred yards; my bullet would be a tumbling mess before I hit my target. Jasper and Lenox were now both in the doorway of the plane, firing. All they had were the junk AKs that we had taken from Al-Harazi's men.

"Give me cover, I'm going close," I yelled to the guys as another volley of gunfire rang out.

So far, the plane had not been hit, but it was a matter of time before this asshole got lucky and we all blew up in the explosion when twenty thousand gallons of kerosene ignited.

I took off in a full sprint across the tarmac, going far right, hoping like hell the shooter was concentrating on the guys and not me. I made it to the other side and slid behind abandoned container boxes. I quickly made my way back in the direction of the shooter. He was hiding under an old tarp, only the barrel of his rifle exposed. I stepped out from behind my hiding spot and popped off two rounds.

The barrel of the rifle now on the ground, I waited a moment before I approached, keeping my weapon trained on the tarp. I gave it a good kick before I reached down to pull it back. An older male with two bullet holes in his neck lay on the ground, dead. Without any further thought, I grabbed his rifle, and with a few hand gestures, I got the okay from Clark to run back to the plane. Jasper, Lenox, Clark, Levi, and Grayson all stood their weapons up, pointing in my direction. I kept my eyes on Levi as I ran, confident they had my six. I wasn't used to working with a team; no one ever had my back. I went in alone, got the job done, and snuck out. I had to admit it was nice knowing I had backup.

"What the fuck was that bullshit?" Levi yelled as we boarded the plane.

"You talking to me?" I asked.

What the hell had his panties in a bunch?

"You got a goddamn death wish, woman?" he continued to yell.

Screw this. "Hell no, I don't. What's wrong,

Levi? You're not used to a woman knowing how to handle her shit? What did you expect me to do? Sit and wait for our only ride home to explode? I saw an opening, and I took it. The shooter was occupied trying to detonate a twenty-thousand-gallon bomb. He wasn't worried about me. Besides, I had five men at my back. I was confident I could take him out."

"Next time you fucking wait. Next time under no circumstances do you take a bullet for me. On second thought, next time stay your ass put," he told me.

"Don't worry, Levi, there won't be a next time." I pushed past him.

"Alright, female version of Rambo, why don't you come over here and let me check your shoulder. That's gonna hurt like a bitch as soon as you stop moving." Clark chuckled and looked at me with something close to humor.

"It's fine. I'll go to the bathroom and clean it off myself."

"Goddamn it," Levi yelled so loud I was surprised the windows hadn't shattered.

Clark followed me to the back of the plane, grabbing a med kit on the way to the small lavatory.

"Don't mind him. His male ego has taken a hit." Clark laughed.

"That's not what I intended," I told him. "I didn't think. I saw the scope and did what I had to do to protect my teammate."

"Is that all he is to you? A teammate?" Clark asked as I took my vest off and pulled my shirt over my head, leaving me standing in front of him with only a bra on.

"He's not even that anymore. The man has hated me for twelve years," I explained.

"If that's what you think, you don't know Levi at all."

I didn't have time to contemplate what Clark meant. I looked up, and Levi was standing there shooting daggers at me. He was one pissed off man.

I squared my shoulders and readied myself for the fight.

CHAPTER THIRTEEN

Levi

I was going to kill my best friend if he made one move to touch Blake. She was standing in front of him in her bra with a bullet hole in her shoulder. A bullet she had taken for me. She had most likely saved my life today and what did I do? I yelled at her. I had never been so scared in my life when she took off across the tarmac. That was bad enough, but knowing she had already been shot and was bleeding had me wanting to come out of my skin. There wasn't a damn thing I could do but stay where I was and provide cover for her. I was going to smack her ass for that stunt later.

Clark motioned for her to turn so he could check the wound. Smart man not touching her.

"No exit wound; we're gonna have to dig the bullet out of you,"

"Copy that Sarge," Blake joked, her eyes moving from me to Clark.

I didn't want her looking at him. "I'll do it," I said.

If anyone was digging a bullet out of Blake, it was me.

"No can do. I'm gonna need you to hold her down; I have nothing to numb her. The faster we do this, the better. She's still high on adrenaline, but as the dump comes, she could go into shock."

"I'll be fine. I've had worse," she said.

Based on the scars on her back, I was afraid she was telling the truth. I wanted to know, but I was afraid to ask. If the person or persons who had tortured her weren't already dead, I was afraid I would commit murder.

Clark opened the med kit and pulled out two saline IVs. He cut one open and poured water over her shoulder to clean off some of the blood. "Are you allergic to anything? Betadine?" he asked.

"No, nothing that I'm aware of," she answered.

Jasper had joined us in the back of the plane with a stack of blankets. "These were all I could find."

"Right here," Clark said and pointed to the aisleway.

Jasper made a bedroll on the floor for Blake to lie on and moved out of the way.

"Let's get this show on the road. Before you lie down, I'm gonna start an IV."

Blake stood while Clark started an IV; the irrational side of me wanted to cover her chest from the rest of my team. I knew no one was looking at her that way, but it still pissed me off my woman was standing in the galley of an aircraft, her breasts partially exposed and a fucking bullet in her shoulder. "Go ahead and lie on your stomach," Clark told her when he finished the IV.

I helped her get on the floor and as comfortable as possible. "Lift your head so I can slide the bag under your cheek." She did as I asked. "Until we can hang the bag and gravity will take over, the weight of your head will put pressure on the bag forcing the solution into the tube," I explained.

Clark quickly pulled out the rest of the instruments he needed and looked at me. "I need you to hold her still," he instructed.

"Copy that."

I allowed myself to personally detach from the

situation and tried to think of her as any other injured soldier. "You ready?" I asked.

She nodded and held my eyes. I saw the moment Clark made his first incision. She gritted her teeth and tears filled her eyes, spilling out of the corners. She remained silent as I held her down, Clark digging in the wound.

"Fuck, I have to cut more, the bastard is too deep. I don't want to stitch up a tear; it won't be so pretty."

"Just do it," she said, and Clark made another cut. This time Blake called out "Fuck!"

I was frozen in place as Blake tried her best to be brave, but her body was shaking, and the tears were flowing freely now. "You're doing great, baby. He's almost got it. Hang in just a minute longer."

"Jasper, use that bag, and clean some of this blood away," Clark instructed.

Jasper got up from the seat and did as Clark asked, wincing when he saw the size of her incision.

"Goddamn, woman. I'd be crying for my mommy if he was digging into me like that. You're doing great."

"Got it," Clark announced and pulled the bloody bullet from her shoulder. "You're lucky as hell it didn't hit the bone."

I held out my hand, and he dropped it in my

palm. I shoved the bullet into my pocket and went back to making sure she remained still.

"Almost done now," I told her.

Jasper poured some more of the saline solution around her wound and opened a package of sterile gauze, pouring a liberal amount of Betadine on the white cotton before handing it to Clark.

"Thanks," he said to Jasper then turned to Blake. "How ya doing?"

"Peachy," she said through gritted teeth. "You better give me a nice clean straight-line, Clark. Don't wanna scare the boys off with another scar."

"I'll do my best, Rambo," Clark laughed.

I wasn't sure why the two of them were joking. He had spent the last ten minutes removing a 7.62 bullet from her flesh. And why the fuck was she joking about making her scar pretty for other men? I didn't want any other man looking at the scar. That scar belonged to me. It was mine, and mine alone.

"Just hurry the fuck up," I growled. I wanted this over so I could take her to a seat and hold her in my arms.

Clark started, and Blake winced. "Holy mother fuck that hurts worse than you cutting me open," she panted in pain.

Twelve stitches later Clark was tying off and

finally cleaning the wound site. "When we get stateside we'll get some antibiotics in you and have my handy work checked. It's gonna leave a scar, but I tried my best."

"I was joking about the scar. One more doesn't matter; trust me. My back has already been shredded all to hell. The good thing is I don't have to see them every day." She gave Clark a tight smile.

"How'd you get them?" Clark asked, and I held my breath.

"An op five years ago in Bogotá. I was chasing down El Demonio and found myself on the business end of his infamous dagger. He held me two days and took his time with me. The worst of what he did to my back scarred. It looks good now compared to what it looked like when I finally got out of there and met up with a Delta team that had been sent in to find me."

"Christ, he was taken out by a member of his own family, right? His wife or sister?" Clark asked.

"That's what the reports say," she chuckled.

"How long before you were able to get back down there?" Clark continued to clean the blood off her shoulder as they talked.

"I never left the country. The guys bandaged me up as good as they could; it looked like he had taken a cheese grater to my back. They gave me a few bags of blood and some fluid and took me back for the raid. I wasn't strong enough to breach the house, but they called me in for the fun stuff. Let's just say that bastard was begging to be sent to hell by the time I was done with him."

I was glad the man was dead and that she had the pleasure to end his miserable existence. El Demonio was known around Bogotá for cutting off fingers or limbs of this enemies. He had been a cartel leader, and a particularly mean one. The name *The Demon* fit him.

"You're all patched up. You did great. I want to leave this IV in. Let's get you to a seat. Levi, you got her? I need to wash up."

"Thanks, Clark." Blake rolled to her side, then to a sitting position. "Hold onto the IV bag, I'll be as gentle as I can," I promised.

Once I had her safely in my arms, I walked to the nearest row of seats and was thankful we were on a private jet with plenty of room. I sat down with her cradled in my arms. "Jasper, can you jimmy-rig this IV up?" I asked and held out the bag, tugging the blanket around her to cover her chest.

Jasper attached the bag to the air vent and looked down at me holding Blake in my arms, a wide smile crossing his face. "Good to see, man," he said and walked to a seat.

I owed Clark for taking such good care of Blake. My hands wouldn't have been steady enough to make a clean incision.

Her eyes were starting to close. "Get some sleep, beautiful. I got you," I whispered.

Blake didn't respond, and within minutes her breathing evened out.

I spent the next three hours staring at the woman in my arms wondering what I was going to do now. Could I forgive her for what she'd done? Could I blame her for a stupid mistake she had made when she was a kid? We were eighteen years old, what the hell did we know? I had been in hell for the last twelve years. Maybe it was time to forget the past and move on.

CHAPTER FOURTEEN

Blake

The moment my eyes opened I felt like I had been run over by a Mac truck. The ache in my shoulder reminded me I had been shot. By way of gunshot wounds, I was lucky. Don't get me wrong; it hurt like a son-of-a-bitch. I thought I was going to throw up the pain was so bad. Thankfully I didn't make a fool of myself and was able to breathe through the worst of it.

Levi was asleep, giving me the perfect opportunity to study his features. He was a good-looking man; perfect chiseled jawline and a strong and commanding presence. He should've been mine; we should've had a family by now. I would've been happy being an Army wife following him wherever we were stationed. How different would my life be if I hadn't been a cocky eighteen-year-old girl thinking I could double-cross Alister Bench? Maybe it was time to swallow my pride and make Levi hear me out. I even had proof if he'd just listen.

I pulled my good arm out from under the blanket he had covered me with and reached up to touch his face. After all these years, I was still in love with this man. My heart still raced when he was near, the electricity still sparked between us as strong as ever. This line of thinking was dangerous. This was how I was going to get my heart shattered a second time. As much as I thought things should've been different, they weren't. I had spent years trying to forget him and finally resigned myself to the truth; I would die loving this man.

I pulled my hand back and closed my eyes. Sleep was my only refuge from the pain.

THE NEXT TIME I woke up I found myself staring into Levi's eyes. "Hey," I croaked out. "Everything alright?"

"I'm sorry I yelled at you earlier. I was scared out

of my fucking mind. Knowing you had been shot was doing crazy things to me," he admitted.

"It's fine. I get it; emotions were high."

"That's an understatement. How do you feel?" he asked.

"It hurts like a bitch."

"We'll get you to a hospital and get you some pain meds soon. We are almost ready to land."

Damn, I had slept the whole trip back to DC, and I noticed my IV had been removed at some point.

"You have to be uncomfortable. Let me move to a seat."

Levi's grip on me tightened, and he held me in place. "You're right where I need you to be. Listen, I was thinking. I'd like to see you again. Maybe I can come up to DC in a few days and spend a weekend up there with you if you have some time." For a second I wondered if Clark had ended up finding some pain meds and I was hallucinating. "If you don't want me to come up, that's fine. Maybe we can start out slow, get to know each other again, talk on the phone some."

"Of course, I want to see you. I guess I just don't understand what's changed. Not that I'm not happy it has."

"Seeing you for starters, watching you take a bullet, remembering all that we were to each other. It got me thinking. It's time to move on, the past is the past, and I need to forgive you and see if what I think we can have is real."

My heart jumped in my chest. One would've thought it was from excitement. Levi was talking to me about a possible future. It was everything I had prayed for. However, it wasn't joy I felt, it was anger and hurt.

I didn't bother asking him to let go of me; I knew he wouldn't. Instead, I pushed myself off his lap and stood, uncaring I was still only in my bra.

"The hell, Blake, be careful. Sit down." Concern and panic laced his tone.

"I don't want or need your forgiveness, Levi. I've tried to tell you, but you wouldn't listen to me. I did nothing wrong, you ass. If you had listened to the voicemails I begged you to, you would've heard everything. Once I realized Alister was trying to bribe me, I recorded the entire conversation. I wanted you to hear it. I wanted to use it to show his investors what a scumbag he was. In that conversation, he called me middle-class trash, he bashed the military, and he tried to blackmail and bribe me. I played along to keep him talking. I pretended I was scared when he threatened to post pictures he had of me in my underwear. I was half nude, Levi. He took pictures off your phone and said he was going to put them on the internet. And you know what? I didn't care. Never once did I even entertain the idea of leaving you." I felt a little dizzy, but I carried on, needing to finally get this off my chest; all of the things I never had a chance to say to him. "The fact that you thought so little of me, that you thought I would take that pig's money over the man I loved is appalling. I wrote to you every single day when you were in basic. I begged you to call me, listen to your voicemail, hear me out. Anything. I begged every single day. You know what I got? Nothing. I've tried to forget you and stop loving you. But I never could. But, you know what? I'm done. You have punished me, *us*, for over a decade for no goddamn reason. You can take whatever apology you think you deserve and your forgiveness and shove them both up your ass. This is goodbye, Levi. At least I have the fucking decency to say those words to you. You didn't even give me that when you walked out on me." I grabbed the blanket off the seat and used my good arm to throw it over my shoulder.

I held on to the top of the chairs as I moved through the aisle to the front of the plane and took a seat in the empty row. The pressure in the cabin had changed, and thankfully we were landing. I couldn't be anywhere near him at the moment. I looked across the aisle and saw Clark looking at me. The pity in his stare told me any hope I'd had that the rest of the team hadn't heard my breakdown was for naught. Christ almighty this trip sucked. My mission was FUBAR, I was an idiot and slept with Levi, I got shot, and the biggest mistake of all was I allowed myself to wish.

I knew better than that.

The moment the plane rolled to a stop and the pilot opened the cabin door I was down the stairs. I sucked in a breath of air and readied myself to face my future – alone.

Suddenly there was a hand on the small of my back. "Come on, let's get you to a doctor to check you out then I'll get you home."

"That's not necessary. I'll be fine," I returned.

All I wanted was to be left alone.

"I'm sure you would be fine, but I'll make sure of it."

"Why are you doing this?" I stopped walking and turned to him.

"You saved my best friend's life," Clark said and put his hand up to stop me from speaking. "And because I respect the hell out of you. You're one hell of an operator and a tough chick."

"Thank you. I don't want to cause issues on your team. You should get back on the plane and go home with them."

I appreciated the gesture, but Levi would be upset if Clark came with me. He already looked like he was ready to kill him on the plane when he was looking at my shoulder.

"Let me tell you a little secret about myself. I don't give a fuck. And Levi would be pissed at me if I *didn't* take care of his woman. You know what he's on that plane doing right now?" Clark asked.

"No."

"He is costing the American taxpayers a mint by tearing that cabin apart trying to get to you. When I left, Jasper was locking his ass down, and it wasn't pretty. Someone is gonna have to explain to Emily why her man's face is busted up, and I'm happy that person will not be me."

I didn't know who this Emily person was, but by the sound of it, she was Jasper's wife or girlfriend. As much as I wanted to say no, I needed the help. My shoulder hurt so damn bad I could barely breathe.

"Thank you." I swayed on my feet, and Clark

steadied me. "I think I need to hurry. I feel like I might pass out."

Clark scooped me up into his arms and started walking toward the hangar. "You know he loves you right?"

"He never came. I waited, but he didn't want me bad enough to fight."

CHAPTER FIFTEEN

Levi

I was in a hell of my own making. I had fucked everything up. Why hadn't I listened to Blake? She was right; I assumed the worst of her that day. I allowed my hatred for Alister and what he'd done to my family to cloud my judgment. I knew better than to think that Blake would betray me. She had always been the best part of me. She was honest and open. Even now, she hadn't let her job close her off to the world. She was still full of light and goodness.

I had been pacing my bedroom for what felt like hours staring at a box that I knew held all the answers. The truth of my past. Not that I needed any proof. I believed Blake when she told me what had happened between her and Alister that day. No, the contents of the box were my punishment; my old phone with all the unread text messages and digital recordings of the voicemails that I never listened to, all the unopened letters she had written me, along with old pictures of us, were sitting in that box waiting for me to face what I had done.

Fuck it! It was time for my reckoning. I could never fix things with Blake if I didn't know the extent of the pain I had caused. This was on me. I had spent years hating the wrong person. She had done nothing wrong; I was the one that had betrayed her.

I opened the box and rummaged through it until I found my old phone and charger. Once I plugged it in, I waited until it had enough power to turn on. Part of me had hoped it was fucked-up and wouldn't turn on, so I didn't have to hear her sweet voice. When the screen came to life, I braced myself for the onslaught of emotions.

I pulled up the first recording and hit play. Alister's voice filled the room. He was offering her a letter of recommendation to a writing camp she had wanted to attend along with an internship at his paper. Blake's voice was skeptical but pleasant. When she thanked him for the offer but turned him down, he switched tactics and offered her money as well. All she had to do was convince me to go to college. She politely turned him down again. Alister then threatened her that he would send pictures of her to message boards and social media sites if she didn't go along, telling her she was already trash and that after the pictures were out, she'd never get into college. She begged him not to do it and told him she would take the money and leave me. She played it off well; she sounded scared as she cried and negotiated with him. I remembered hearing this part of the conversation.

My weekly Army DEP meeting had ended early, and I had rushed home to shower and change so I could go see Blake. When I pulled up to the house, I was excited she was there waiting for me. When I walked in, I heard voices in Alister's study. I stood outside the door and listened to Blake talking to Alister about paying off her parent's house, and he would transfer the money after she had convinced me to go to college. She promised him she'd never see me again. Thinking back, I remembered she was crying. In my anger, her tears hadn't registered. I was so mad I stomped to the front door, making sure I'd slammed it as loud as possible so they'd hear.

Shame washed over me. Why hadn't I stayed? All I had to do was go into the study and confront Alister. Instead, I ran like a coward.

I moved on to the next recording. Blake was crying, begging me to meet her at our spot. She was already there waiting for me.

The next was her asking me where I was, that she wanted to ask me what she should do with the recording she had made, explaining she had sent it to me and emailed it to herself so if Alister tried to get her phone, it was multiple places.

I chuckled to myself. Even at eighteen, Blake was already every bit super sleuth reporter.

From then on, each message got more and more desperate, asking where I was. With each message the panic grew in her voice, begging me to listen to the recording.

She filled my voicemail box, twenty messages in all before my phone would no longer accept more. I scrolled through the text messages. They were the same as the voicemails. She was scared, wanted to know where I was, how much she loved me, that I had to hear her out. Over and over she asked me to listen to her.

By the time I had sorted through the letters, putting them in chronological order, I was spent, completely and totally raw. When I stared at her pretty handwriting on the envelope, my heart filled with dread. There was no way I'd ever be able to fix this. How would she ever forgive me for the heartache I had caused?

I gently tore open the envelope, not wanting to destroy what was most likely the last words I'd ever have from her.

Dear Levi,

You left! I don't know if Sergeant Williams told you, but I went down to the recruit station and begged for him to tell me when your flight was so I could say goodbye. But, he wouldn't tell me. I wanted to see you so bad before you left.

I miss you!

Have you listened to the voicemails I left? Please listen to them; they explain everything. I know you heard what I said to Alister. It wasn't what you thought. I promise! You know I would never lie to you. The voicemail explains everything. I'm sorry you heard what you did, I know it sounded bad. I don't blame you for leaving the house. But I swear to you, I would never leave you. I love you, Levi.

I'm still planning on moving wherever you're stationed. I haven't accepted any offers for college in the fall. My parents agree I should wait until we're settled and do some community college classes and reapply to local schools next year. Does that work for you? I can pick up a part-time job, too. We'll make it work.

There's not a day that goes by that I don't think about you and miss you. I love you so much! Please write me back soon. Mom and Dad wanted me to tell you that they miss you, too, and are proud of you. I am, too. I hope you're doing well.

Please write me back soon,

Yours forever,

Blake

There were no words for how big of a dick I was. Even after I had left her without a goodbye, she still planned on following me. I couldn't believe she held off her first year of college for me, for us. My self-disgust knew no bounds.

I spent the rest of the night reading every word of every letter. Her final words to me were like a knife in my chest.

Dear Levi,

I suppose this will be my last letter to you. With basic graduation next week and you leaving for AIT, I will no longer have a way to contact you.

I'm truly sorry that in my haste and foolish plan I lost you. I was stupid to think I could go against Alister Bench and come out a winner. If nothing else,

I hope you believe that I never did take a dime of his money.

You have made it clear that you no longer want me to be a part of your life. As hard as it is, I will respect your wishes. I want you to know that I loved every minute we were together. Over the last two years, you have taught me so much about myself. I was a shy, lonely girl when you first found me on the tailgate of Lynn's pickup truck in the parking lot of the Tastee-Freez. Because of you, I'm now a confident, strong young woman. Thank you for teaching me to believe in myself. I will forever be grateful you loved me.

I'm so proud you followed your heart. I know you were meant for great things and you will serve with commitment and honor. I'm only sorry I will not be by your side to watch.

I hope you find all the happiness you deserve.
Good Luck,
Blake

Fuck! I had to fix this. I grabbed my cell off my nightstand, uncaring it might be too late to call.

"I need her address," I told Clark when he answered.

CHAPTER SIXTEEN

Blake

The first letter came about a week after I got home from Oman. It sat on my kitchen table for another few days like a snake threatening to strike each time I walked by it. When I added the second, then the third, to the pile, I wondered if I should open them. By the time I had five they had started to come every day. Why was he doing this now? I had finally made peace with the knowledge that I was never meant to be with Levi. Now he was torturing me. Five letters sat on my table, and I was thankful it was Sunday, and a new one wouldn't be delivered.

My phone chimed, and I checked the notifications, smiling when I saw it was from Clark.

Clark: How's the boo-boo, Rambo?

Me: Ass! The stitches are itchy, leaving me to wonder why the medic didn't just glue me up instead of giving me a zipper.

Clark: Wanted it to look pretty for you. Glue would've scarred worse.

Me: Here I thought it was because you missed your sewing circle with the old bittys.

Clark: They stopped inviting me when they needed to double up on their blood pressure meds because I'm super-hot.

I threw my head back and laughed.

Me: In your dreams. The incision is great. No infection. Thanks again.

Clark: Good, then you're ready for an op.

I wished! I still wasn't cleared for field work, so I had been stuck behind a desk.

Me: Desk duty another two weeks.

Clark: You misunderstood. I wasn't asking *if* you were ready. I'm telling you that you're on an op. You leave tomorrow.

Me: WTF. I didn't get orders. Wait, how do you know that?

Clark: You'll have all the intel within the hour. See you soon.

Me: Explain.

Clark: Unsecured. Out.

Me: Copy that.

What just happened? I looked at the letters and wondered if Levi had sent me mission orders. That was a silly notion that the CIA or Army would use snail mail, but it sounded like a good excuse to use to open the envelopes. I could lie to myself and pretend I had to open them up for work. I was getting better at that these days. Each day I woke up and told myself a lie. Everything was fine. I didn't miss him. I was over him. I was better off without him. I didn't love him.

I figured for now if that was what I needed to get through my day, I was going to give it to myself. I would fake it until I made it. That was the saying, right? One day this pain would dull. It had once before.

I swiped the letters off the table and walked to the couch, contemplating if I should switch out my coffee for whiskey. Depending on what these letters said, I might need something stiff.

I stared at the envelope, hoping that it would be a clue as to its contents. The perfect sharp penmanship gave nothing away.

I opened it and pulled out the lined loose-leaf paper.

My Sweet Blake,

It has taken me entirely too long to answer your letters. I saved every one you wrote me while I was in basic. I'm ashamed to say, I only opened them tonight. I've read every one of them. As a matter of fact, I have every love note you ever wrote me, every photo, most of the movie ticket stubs, lots of things that seem insignificant individually, but all together they tell the story of us.

I've kept them with me all these years. I hadn't opened the box in years, but I felt some measure of peace knowing I had a part of us with me.

First – I'm sorry for a lot of things. Most of all I'm sorry I didn't trust in us - in you. I let my self-doubt that I wasn't good enough for you, along with my anger toward Alister, rule my emotions. If I had thought about what I was doing, I would've known that you could never betray me, or anyone for that matter. It is not in your nature to be underhanded or deceitful. My actions hurt you, and I apologize for that.

I listened to your voice messages and read your text messages. (I saved my old phone as well.) I need you to understand; I didn't listen to those messages because I needed proof or I didn't believe you. I listened because I deserved all the pain it caused me when I heard the anguish in your voice. Hearing you cry, knowing I had done that to you, was like a thousand shards of glass slicing my heart.

I have done many things in my life I'm not proud of, some I'm deeply ashamed of, but none of them come close to the mortification I feel at this moment. The pain I have caused you is abhorrent and unforgivable. I understand that now. I understand the gravity of my actions and how they altered both of our lives.

We should've been celebrating wedding anniversaries and the births of our children. Instead, I've spent those years mourning the loss of a love I tossed away.

Thank you for your letters while I was in basic. I may not have opened them, but they helped me. Knowing that there was one person back home that thought of me got me through some hard times, even when I didn't deserve it.

I love you, Blake.

I've loved you since the day I finally got up the nerve to talk to you that night at the Tastee-Freez. But you have to know, I loved the thought of you long before then. I don't think I ever told you this, but the *first day of freshman year when I saw you walk in English class, I nearly fell out of my seat. I asked you if I could borrow a pen. (I had plenty.) However, I had to know if the sound of your voice was as sweet as your smile. When it was, when the sweet melody hit my soul, I knew you were too good for me. I spent the next two years watching you, wishing I could have you.*

I didn't get to tell you before you left but I'm so damn proud of the woman you grew up to be. You're brave and tough, and I hate to sound like a douche here, but hot as hell when you're in the field taking care of business. You're one hell of an agent with good instincts.

Please be safe out there, Blake, and if you ever need someone to have your back I'm here – no strings, no questions asked. I will not push you for more, but if there is ever a time you think you can forgive me – I'll be waiting.

Yours forever,

-L

By the time I was done reading his letter I didn't know what to do. I held four more letters in my hand, and I was afraid to open them. What if in the next letter he took back everything he had said. Wasn't this everything I had wanted? It was times like this I wish I had a friend. I worked in a department with all men. We were co-workers, not going-out buddies. I was friendly with some of the wives, but not close enough to spill my guts to about boy problems.

There was only one person I could talk to.

Me: Can I call you?

CHAPTER SEVENTEEN

Levi

It had been two weeks since I started writing Blake. A letter a day, just like she did when I was in basic. Each day I pulled out a new letter and answered any of the questions she had asked. Some were simple like how was the food or what kind of room did I bunk in. Other times she asked questions like did I still love her or how could I have left her so easily. Those were harder to answer – but I did, with complete honesty and vulnerability. She deserved to know the truth, even if it hurt to tell her.

She had not answered a single letter, not that I expected her to. I had a lot to make up for.

"Did you come up with anything?" Jasper asked.

"Huh?"

"Where the hell did you just go?" Clark laughed.

"Sorry. What did you ask?" Clark ignored me and pulled his phone out of his pocket and smiled. He'd been doing that a lot lately.

"I gotta take this call, be right back." He put his phone up to his ear and walked out of the office.

"Did you find anything on the oil company?" Jasper elaborated.

There had been chatter about an INCONUS terror plot, and an oil company name had been mentioned as well. We were trying to see if there was a link between the two.

"Yeah, it's back at the hangar. I think I found a loose connection," I told him.

Clark came back into the room with a broad smile on his face. "The commander needs us at the hangar."

"And that is cause for a smile?" I asked.

"Sure. I'm a bright and sunny kinda guy. What can I say?"

Lenox nearly spit his soda out while Jasper and I couldn't hold back the laughter.

"Holy shit, that was hilarious. Bright and sunny? What the hell? You been stashin' a woman at your place? You've been in a good mood these last few weeks, you getting' laid?" Jasper laughed.

Come to think of it, he had been in a good mood, and there has been a bunch of text messaging going on.

"You gotta woman, brother?" I asked.

"Yes, to one of the three questions. You ass wipes ready to go?" he asked, his smile fading.

The car ride over to the hangar was spent going over what I had found about the oil company. Jasper was telling me a funny story about Jason when we walked into the hangar, and I froze.

Blake.

What the hell was she doing here? She looked fucking gorgeous standing next to the commander in a tight knee-length skirt and a pair of fuck-me pumps – and I would gladly do just that as soon as I could get her alone.

"Ladies. Nice of you to make it. I think you all know Agent Blake Porter," the commander said.

I glanced up to look at Blake. I had been so stuck on her shoes I hadn't noticed that she was frowning at me.

"The CIA was nice enough to loan Blake to us. She'll be at the 707 for the foreseeable future," he continued.

The guys all said hello and welcomed her like a long-lost friend. Clark had a wide shit-eating grin that I was trying to understand. Something wasn't right. I looked between her and Clark one more time and felt my temper rise. I cut my eyes to Blake, and her frown deepened.

The commander, not paying attention to the tension in the room, made his way to the door. "Blake, it's a pleasure to have you. I trust that Clark has got you settled and if you need anything else the team will take care of you."

There it was, the confirmation I needed. Clark had been taking care of her. I needed to hold my shit together for about ten more minutes until I had enough time to gather my shit and tell the commander I needed a transfer. I had zero issue going to a line unit as long as it meant I didn't have to see Clark and Blake cozied up together.

"Thank you, sir. It's a pleasure to be on the team," she replied.

The door closed behind the commander, and Clark turned to me, a hard look on his face.

"Outside," he demanded.

"Absolutely."

Without another word, I headed for the door and didn't bother holding it open for Clark. I had my fist cocked back ready to punch the wall when Clark stepped outside.

"I wouldn't do that, brother."

"Would you rather it be you, *brother*," I growled.

"You need to stop and think. Don't do this to yourself or to her again. I don't know what it is about that woman that makes you lose your ever-loving mind, but you need to think long and hard about the next words you're going to say to her. You and I, we're brothers, we can get over anything. That woman in there just took a huge leap of faith, and if you break her heart again, she'll be gone. For good this time," he warned.

"She's been staying with you?" I asked.

"No. She's at the base hotel," he answered.

"That place is a piece of shit. How could you let her stay there?"

The base hotel was nothing short of a rent-by-the-night frat house. Young boys that live in the barracks rent a hotel room when they want to bring a girl back to base but don't want the hassle of getting busted with a girl in their room.

"Seriously. That woman scares me a little. She can handle herself just fine. Cool your jets and go talk to her."

"I lose my shit around her. I can't seem to stop doing it. I'm completely unreasonable when it comes to Blake Porter," I admitted. "I'm sorry. I know better than to think you'd take my girl."

"Oh, I'd take her in a heartbeat - if she wasn't yours. I've never loved a woman like you love Blake, not even my own wife. How fucked up is that? When I caught her and my little brother in bed, I was more pissed my own blood would turn on me than I was that she had fucked another man. I haven't missed her a single day since I got shot of her ass."

"Thanks for watching out for her."

I didn't wait for Clark to reply. Blake was less than two hundred yards away from me, and I had wasted enough time.

When I entered the hangar, Jasper and Lenox were showing her the cage where we kept our gear, and I paused to fully take her in. She looked so out of place in a sexy pair of heels and business attire, walking around dirty gear and night vision devices. She laughed at something Lenox said, and my heart jumped in my chest. I was not going to fuck this up.

I moved to her, grabbed her hand, and without a word I tugged her out of the cage, through the cavernous space and straight out the door. I didn't give zero fucks my team was howling with laughter.

"Are you here for good?" I asked as we walked up to the SUV we drove over in.

"Depends," she answered.

"On?"

She wasn't going back to Virginia, or if she was, I was out. I'd gladly give everything up for our second chance.

"Your next words." She cocked her hip out, her hand going there, and a sassy smile graced her beautiful face.

I did what came naturally, what felt right.

I drop to my knee in front of her.

"Marry me."

"Was that a question, Levi McCoy?" she laughed.

"Not unless you need it to be," I told her.

"Yes."

"Yes to what?" Before I stood, I needed clarification.

"Yes. I feel like I've been waiting my whole life to hear you say those words. A hundred times, yes."

I got to my feet and pulled her into my arms.

"Right now, Blake. I want to go right now and make you my wife. No more waiting. I cannot wait one more day to finally be your husband."

"Are you crazy?" she laughed.

"Yes. I've been told that I lose my mind when I'm around you. It's true, but I have to say this is the most rational idea I've ever had."

"He is totally insane when it comes to you," Jasper's nosey ass said from behind me. "So, do you two need a ride to the courthouse? Don't think you two are getting hitched without the team there."

"Looks like we're getting married, boys," Blake called out, shaking her head at me. "If you ever think about leaving me again, just remember I have perfect aim and am well-trained on a variety of high-powered weapons."

"Noted."

And after twelve agonizing years, I finally kissed her. When her tongue came out to meet mine, she tasted just like I remembered, sweet like honey.

"I love you, baby," I whispered when I broke the kiss.

"I love you, Levi."

CHAPTER EIGHTEEN

Blake

We got married that afternoon in an unremarkable ceremony by the Justice of the Peace in a boring courtroom. It was perfect. I was surrounded by a group of extraordinary men, and their women, as I married the most remarkable, unforgettable man I'd ever known. I didn't need the flourish of a big wedding, all I wanted was Levi McCoy. And when the Justice of the Peace pronounced us husband and wife, I felt like the scale that was my life was finally balanced. We made it. It took a while, but we made our way back to each other.

We won.

The seven of us were standing outside the courtroom near the parking lot when Lily, Lenox's wife, announced we were celebrating at their house tonight. I tried to protest, being that she was pregnant with a one-year-old at home. I told her we could wait and have some catered event later so she didn't have to worry about playing hostess.

"Good luck convincing my wife she can't have a party," Lenox chuckled.

"I don't want to impose," I explained.

"Family is never an imposition," Emily, Jasper's fiancé, told me.

"Is that alright with you?" I asked Levi.

"Whatever you want to do, baby, I'm good."

Clark sighed an over-exaggerated groan. "Great. Another one has handed over his manhood."

"As long as you're sure. I'd love to spend time with you all."

Lily and Emily both seemed really great; I couldn't wait to get to know them better – and their kids, too.

"Perfect. Emily and I will take care of everything. I'm so excited," Lily beamed.

"I'm taking my wife home before we come over," Levi announced and I about jumped up and down hearing him call me that.

"That will give Lily time to hide the knives from Rambo." Everyone turned and stared at Clark.

"What? The chick is crazy scary with a knife. I've seen her handy work first hand."

"Can you please have one family gathering without talking about fighting, fucking, or killing? Just one?" Lily whined.

The guys all laughed at what must've been an inside joke, and I felt Levi's lips at my ear. "Are you ready to go home?" he asked.

Home.

"So ready. Are we picking up my stuff now? I only have a suitcase, and it's packed ready to go," I told him.

The rest of the contents of my apartment were being shipped down, courtesy of the CIA relocation allotment.

"Is that so? All packed up?" he teased.

"What can I say? I was hopeful," I said with a smile.

"We're leaving."

Levi didn't wait for the guys to say goodbye as he drug me across the lot to his truck. This one was different than the one he had in high school but no less cool. It might not have had the modified loud exhaust all the teenage boys had, but it was jacked up and pretty. He helped me up before he rounded the hood and got behind the wheel.

Before we pulled out of the lot, an old Hunter Hayes song started to play. When the first keys of "Wanted" started to come through the speakers, he turned it up. And the moment his smooth sexy voice hit my ears, the memories rushed back. But this was no longer about the past. We had a future. I cocked myself sideways to get a better view and goosebumps broke out over my arms. Every so often he would take his eyes off the road and glance at me, his golden eyes heated as he belted out the words of the song. His head swayed in perfect rhythm, and his hand was strumming on the steering wheel.

So damn sexy.

When the chorus hit, I felt every word he was singing deep in my soul. He made me feel like that song was written just for us. He did that with every song he sang. It was like he believed the words, he felt the music. When he licked his lips between verses, I couldn't take my eyes off of them. When he bit his bottom lip, it sent chills to all the right places. I heard him chuckle before he picked back up the lyrics and kept going. Yeah, he'd caught me. I couldn't bring myself to care nor could I stop studying his profile, his sexy jawline, full sexy lips, the slope of his nose. I'd had this man every way a woman could. I'd given him my virginity when I was a teenager, but as I sat in his truck listening to him, I felt like I was seeing him for the first time. When the last of the song played, he was pulling to the main gate and lowered the volume.

"Baby, you have to stop looking at me like that," he said as he rolled down his window and handed his ID to the MP.

The MP waved us through, and I asked, "Like what?"

"Maybe you're not looking at me any particular way. It's just you. When you look at me, I feel like I'm the best version of myself."

"I hope you always feel that way. I love watching you sing to me."

Some emotion flashed across his face, but he quickly masked it and ignored my comment. "We're here. What floor are you on?" he asked.

I gave him directions to the room and handed him my room key. He was back to the truck, suitcase in hand, within minutes. On the drive back to his apartment he told me stories about Lily and Lenox and her getting caught up with a guy named Roman. I'd helped to gather intel on him, but I had no idea what agency was using the information. When he told me that they were also high school friends my heart clenched. They had only been back together again going on two years, and they were working on baby number two. Jasper and Emily were planning on getting married later in the month.

We pulled into a nice apartment complex, the exterior was beautiful and well kept. Very different than the downtown high-rise I'd been living in. I like this much better. There were trees all around and green grass. His building was around back; these looked more like townhouses with attached garages.

"Before we go in, I wanted to talk to you about something," I told him.

"Everything alright?" he asked, his attention now on me.

"Everything is perfect. I wanted to say this to clear the air. Today when you walked in and saw me, and the commander mentioned Clark helping me... you know that..."

"You don't need to say it. I trust you. I was just shocked to see you at first. Right before we went over to the hangar, I was thinking about the letters, wondering if you were even reading them, not blaming you if you weren't. All I've thought about since I got home was how I was going to fix what I had done. And, maybe I was a little jealous. Clark has been walking around smiling and texting a bunch. When I found out you were the person he was texting, I was a little jealous. I missed you. I wanted to be the one talking to you."

"When your first letter came I was too afraid to open it. I had five letters before I started reading them. After I read the first one, I knew what I wanted to do, but I needed someone to tell me I wasn't crazy. Clark was the only one I felt comfortable talking to. All the times before that, he was simply checking on *Levi's girl* as he put it."

"What did you want to do?" he asked.

"Come straight here. Clark had already been sneaky and put a bug in the commander's ear about me and was trying to maneuver me on one of your ops. When I called him and said I wanted to come and I was putting in for a transfer, or I was handing in my resignation, he told me he was confident the commander wanted me. It turns out he was right. It took a little longer than I wanted to get down here."

Levi smiled a sad smile and shook his head. "He is always the one in the background making sure that everyone is happy, but he refuses to move on himself."

"He's not ready. He says that it doesn't bother him, but he doesn't trust women. I suspect that you guys are the only ones he truly trusts. I don't blame him. What his wife and brother did to him is screwed up."

"He told you about them?"

Oh hell. I hoped I didn't just cause a problem. "He did. Is that okay?"

"Yeah. I'm happy he told you. You're right, he doesn't trust, and if he told you that story, it means he trusts you more than you realize. That's a good thing. You ready to go in now?"

"Oh yeah, more than ready."

"One more thing. Those shoes are sexy as fuck, and you will be wearing them for me another night when I can throw those sexy legs over my shoulders. But today, I want to enjoy my wife nice and slow."

CHAPTER NINETEEN

Levi

"Ohmigod!" Blake breathed against my neck. Her legs locked tight around the small of my back; her hips tipped up giving me the perfect angle to thrust deep.

We had walked into the house and straight into the bedroom. I might've pointed to the kitchen on our way back, but I cannot recall for certain. I was on a mission with a singular thought to get my wife to bed.

I had taken my time working her up with my hands and mouth, ignoring her grunts and whines of protest when I wouldn't speed things along. I wanted to taste every inch of her, and I did. There was no place I hadn't sucked and kissed before I finally settled between her thighs. This time, unlike in Oman, I kissed her sweet and long as I pushed inside. There was no mistaking I was making love to her. It didn't matter that it was wild and energetic, and there was groping and squeezing; every last bit of it was pure love.

Her arms snaked around my back, and she fisted my hair, tugging my head back. I gave her my eyes, and she panted, "I love you."

I closed my eyes and let her words settle over my body. I fought back the guilt and pain, but there was no room in our bed for those things. We were starting over, and I had the chance to right all of my wrongs. We would never get back those years, but that no longer mattered.

Today was now, and she was mine.

"I love you, Blake. So goddamn much."

I set a ruthless pace, her hips coming up to meet my thrusts, and when her nails scraped down my back, I felt the first signs of my orgasm fast approaching.

I planted my elbow next to her head and balanced, letting my other hand move over her heated skin down to her clit. Her hips bucked, her head thrashed side to side, and she let out a long sexy moan. When the last of her orgasm faded I planted deep, heat snaked up my spine, my balls tightened, and white-hot pleasure exploded.

"Blake," I groaned.

I rolled us to the side, keeping the connection. With the sweet smell of sex lingering in the room, I took Blake in, her flushed skin, her dazed eyes, the rapid rise and fall of her chest. How did I get so damn lucky? I wanted to fall at this woman's feet and thank her for loving me.

She brushed her sweaty hair from her face and with a wicked smile she asked, "Do we have time for a shower?"

"I know that smile," I told her.

"You got to play. It's only fair. I want you to feel good, too," she pouted.

Blake was quite possibly the only woman in the universe that would pout because I hadn't let her touch me. I wanted today to be all about her. Again, how did I get so lucky?

"Baby, if that felt any better I would've passed out," I explained.

"You know what I mean."

I kissed her forehead and rolled again, so she was on top of me. "I'm all yours. You can take whatever you want." She swiveled her hips, and I bit back a curse.

"Now you have me conflicted," she moaned and rocked back.

"About?"

"Well... do I want this?" She paused and lifted herself gliding up my still hard dick. "Or do I want to take you in the shower and taste you?" She slid back down. "Both would be so good." Up she went again. "But I haven't tasted you in so long." And she slammed herself down.

My fingers dug into her hip, and I held her still. "You're killing me. You have two point five seconds to make up your mind before I do it for you."

The visual alone was enough to make me want to come again. She was magnificent sitting on my lap, her tits swaying, her toned thighs squeezing my legs all the way down to where we were connected. She had to make up her mind, and fast.

"Shower," she said and pulled off me.

I let out a long exhale before knifing up to follow her. Yeah, she was going to kill me. I was watching her ass sway as she walked and that's when I noticed it. I couldn't help staring at my come as it ran down her inner thigh. Some deep, fucked-up excitement that made me feel like beating my chest like a caveman washed over me. Now the shower didn't seem like such a good idea. I didn't want her to wash it away. Before I could pull myself from my stupor, she was already in the shower.

When I stepped in behind her, she turned and welcomed me with a kiss. Not a sweet, gentle one like we had shared in bed; she was consuming me, taking what she wanted, and I denied her nothing. Small, soft hands roamed my body, washing me while I stood frozen in place, mesmerized. Amazed that Blake was really here. I hoped I never got over this feeling of excitement and wonder. I had longed for this, wanted her back for so long.

She dropped to her knees in front of me. "This might not be very good." She spoke so softly I could barely hear her over the rushing water.

I thought she was joking. Blake knew how to give me head; she was a master at it. However, the shy timid look on her face told me she wasn't.

"Come here," I told her.

I was not having a conversation with her on her knees in front of me. She stood up, and I pulled her to me. "What's wrong?"

"It's just that I..." She paused and looked down at my chest.

"Look at me. You what?" She shook her head and continued to look down. "Baby. Please look at me."

When she did, there was doubt in her eyes. "It's

been a long time. I might not remember how to do it."

"Blake," I started.

"No. I want to, really want to. But it might not be any good this time."

"Baby." I smiled. "Practice all you like," I chuckled.

"Okay. You've been warned." She smiled back at me.

She dropped back to her knees and went about torturing me. She practiced alright. She practiced using her tongue to trace the throbbing vein down the underside of my dick. She took her time to get reacquainted with the engorged head while she kissed and sucked it. By the time she had finally taken me fully in her mouth she had me breathless, panting out her name as she took me deep.

I held her hair back, giving me a perfect view as my dick tunneled in and out of her mouth. I was getting ready to beg her to finish me off when she used her fingernail to tickle my balls before she held them in a firm but gentle grip. I let my head fall back, breaking the erotic sight in an effort to enjoy the pleasure a moment longer.

"I'm gonna come, baby," I warned.

Her grip tightened on my balls, and her other

hand went to my ass. Blake's nails dug in, and she pulled me into her, forcing my dick deeper down her throat. My hands flexed trying my hardest not to hold her there.

"Blake, baby, that is so fucking good." She bobbed up and down faster, swallowing my entire dick to the root. "Now. I'm gonna come right... now," I moaned and shot off in her mouth. I watched as she swallowed what she could, the rest leaking out the corner of her mouth.

She pulled off my dick with a pop and sat back on her heels, licking my come off her lips. "Holy shit, that has to be the sexiest fucking thing I've ever seen."

She smiled up at me, and that was when I realized how wrong I had been. Blake smiling at me with love and mischief dancing in her eyes was way better.

"You're so beautiful, Blake." I held my hand out to her, pulling her up and into my chest. I breathed her in and held her close.

Blake McCoy was all mine.

Now all that was left was to ask her when she wanted to start filling the house with babies.

CHAPTER TWENTY

Blake

It had only been two hours, but I felt like I'd known this group for years. They all welcomed me into the family without thought or reservation. Lily and Emily had even picked up a small wedding cake for us. I loved the neighborhood Lily and Lenox lived in. Their house was nice, but it was the large backyard I loved. There were more toys outside than one child could possibly play with and a monstrosity of a swing set. When I asked Lily about it, she rolled her eyes, and Emily laughed.

They told me the story of the day the guys built it. They had sat outside on the deck and watched the guys carry the lumber into the backyard, shirtless, and thanked the hot Georgia weather for being so humid. Lenox growled when he heard this and told Levi, Jasper, and Clark they were not to take their shirts off in front of his wife. That sucked for me; it seemed I would never get the pleasure of the show. Not that I needed it anyway. I had Levi, and that was more than enough.

Lily, Emily and I were in the backyard watching Jason help a toddling Carter walk around the grass when Lily turned to me and asked, "Did you really get shot saving Levi?"

"I thought you didn't like to talk about fighting, fucking, or killing," Emily laughed.

"I said I didn't want to talk about that with the guys. Not my girls. Spill sister." Lily turned in her seat to look at me, her pregnant belly protruding under her shirt like a perfect little basketball.

"I wouldn't call it saving. I just so happened to see the reflection of the scope before anyone else."

"CIA, huh?" Emily said.

"Yes, I was recruited while I was in college. I've been in the field eight years now."

"So, are you still going to be in the field now that you and Levi are married?" Lily shyly asked.

"We haven't talked about it," I admitted. "For

now, I'm embedded with the 707. I will deploy with them. Or that was the plan. The commander might pull me now that we're married. Even though I'm not in the military, the government frowns on spouses working for the same command. I would like to stay with the 707 if they'll let me. But honestly, I think I'm done with fieldwork. I want to start having babies."

"Jesus. Before we know it this place will be overrun with rug rats. We already have two and a half counting that half-baked bun in her oven," Clark said from the doorway, pointing at Lily. There was something in the way that Clark joked about kids that gave me the impression that he was a little jealous. Clark was the oldest of the group at thirty-six, and he had no kids.

Lenox, Jasper, and Levi had joined us on the deck as well. While the other men had moved to sit around the large table, Levi remained standing, staring at me. I studied his expression, trying to figure out what he was thinking. The corner of his mouth tipped up, and he asked, "You wanna have my babies?"

"Of course, I do," I told him.

"Now?" he asked.

"What is it with you and that word?" I laughed.

"Please not now. I want to enjoy my steak and as happy as I am you two lovebirds are back together, I don't want to watch you make a baby," Clark said and made a gagging sound.

I was getting ready to comment on Clark's immature comment when Lily beat me to it.

"Lame," she said and threw one of the carrots off her plate in his direction.

"It's because I wasted too many years. I want everything right now," Levi answered.

This was a strange time to be having this conversation in front of everyone, but no one seemed to find it out of the ordinary.

"Levi McCoy, I have dreamt of havin' your babies since I was a starry-eyed teenager watching you play football, thinking you were the hottest quarterback that ever was. And I have loved you just as long. But all that? That is gone. We are finally free of our past, and from now on, we are only lookin' ahead. And it is bright and happy and filled with family and good friends. You wanna start having those babies now? I'm ready."

That was the truth of it; we were free.

"You going to get that thingy out?" he asked.

There was nothing I could do but smile. I thought about choking him for talking about my IUD in front of everyone. However, the hopeful look on his face saved him.

"Sure. You want to come sit down and eat?" I asked, hoping he got the hint and didn't ask any more questions.

After Levi sat, we all laughed more than we ate, each guy trying to one-up the other on embarrassing stories. They had Lily, Emily and I in tears with their antics. Sometimes their stories involved hand gestures or full body movements that required them to stand to act out a part of the story. They were all comfortable around each other, close as brothers could be. I loved that Levi had that. His birth family sucked, and I was happy he'd been able to make a new one. A family of *his* own making, one that was loyal and caring.

After Lily went upstairs to put Carter to sleep, Emily and I cleaned up the kitchen. I could hear the guys talking to Jason in the other room about teaching him to play baseball, and I smiled. I loved knowing that one day, my son or daughter would have three uncles that would love and protect him or her.

"What's that smile for?" Emily asked.

"Just listening to Jason and the guys. He is a great kid," I told her.

"Thanks. He's a good boy." She looked like she was going to say more when Jasper came into the kitchen.

"Em, sweetheart, Reagan texted me and said she'd be passing through Georgia in the next few weeks and wanted to know if it was alright to stop by."

"Yes. I'd love to meet her. Ask her if she can stay a few days. I want her to meet the girls, and we'll take her shopping for her new job. It will be her graduation gift since we can't make it to Montana."

"Meet who?" Levi asked, joining us in the kitchen as well.

"Reagan, Liz's sister," Emily told Levi.

"Oh." Levi cut his eyes to Jasper, and when I followed his gaze, Jasper was still looking at Emily. I couldn't figure out what the big deal was, or who Liz was because Jasper just looked like – Jasper.

"I hope she can stay a few days," Emily continued. "You guys are all going to love her. She is super sweet. I've gotten to know her over text and phone calls. We wanted to go to her graduation, but you guys have work-ups next week, and Jasper couldn't get leave," she explained.

Levi looked back at me and discreetly shook his head. "You ready to go?" he asked.

Lily came back down, and we all said our good-byes with the promise I'd come back and hang out with her and Emily again soon. On the car ride back to *our* place, as Levi corrected when I called it his, he told the story of Jasper, Liz, and their daughter Alesha. My heart broke for Jasper. I was happy he was able to let go of his past and find happiness with Emily and Jason. I had a whole new respect for Emily. The woman was kind to her core, welcoming Liz's sister, Reagan, into their home. But more than that, she wanted to pull her into the fold and make her family. Jasper lucked out finding Emily.

By the time we made it home, I was exhausted and ready for bed. Levi had cleared out some drawers for me to use until we figured out what we were going to do about furniture. Being as I was too tired to unpack, I was also too tired to rummage through my suitcase to find something to wear. I pulled open one of Levi's drawers, and there was a stack of the letters I had written him. There were also pictures of us from high school, movie ticket stubs, concert tickets - our history. As I moved the items around, I found a mangled fragmented 7.62 bullet and picked it up.

Levi came up behind me and wrapped his arms around me.

"You saved it?" I asked.

"Yes." His arms tightened around me.

"Why?"

"Baby, you took that bullet for me. I watched as Clark pulled that out of your flesh. A bullet that had my name on it. But instead, you stepped in front of it, and more than likely saved my life." He kissed the top of my head and locked eyes with me in the mirror that hung above the dresser. "Jasper, Clark, and Lenox are a little superstitious. Each of them has a .308 round they carry with them when we deploy. It is always somewhere on their person. The round has their name engraved on the bullet. The thought is, if they have the bullet with their name on it in their pocket, they'll be safe. I was the only one that didn't carry one." He turned the bullet over in my hand. "Now I have one. One that my wife gave me."

McCoy was etched into the copper.

"You'll take this with you when you deploy," I told him.

"I'll never leave home without it. Unless you need it."

His eyes held mine. I guess that was his way of asking without asking.

"Levi, I love my job. I'm a good agent, and I'm excellent in the field. In the last eight years, I bet I've been out almost as much as you have. However, I haven't lost sight of how I was recruited and what my driving force has been all these years. I promised myself I would destroy Alister Bench. And now, I have everything to do just that. The arrest warrant came down earlier today. We are ready to take him down. I'm telling you that to tell you this. I'm ready to be done. I will stay with the 707 as logistics and information gathering. If the agency has an issue with that, I'll quit. I have accomplished everything I set out to do with them."

"I want to go with you when you take down Bench," Levi said, his tone dark and menacing.

"I didn't doubt you would. The team can't go, it's an INCONUS takedown. The commander okayed your presence in a non-official capacity.

"You're the perfect wife." He smiled at me.

"Why is that?"

"Because you're totally hot when you carry a gun and use acronyms like INCONUS. And baby, this might piss you off, but you also give world class head."

I busted out laughing. "You're so sweet. You certainly know the way to a woman's heart." I rolled my eyes.

"Would you prefer if I told you that there is not

another woman that I could begin to compare to you. That when I look at you, I'm reminded of all that is right in the world. That I missed you every day. That I knew I would never have a family because I could never love another woman. That I think you're the smartest most beautiful woman I've ever known. Because baby, if you need to hear that, I'll tell you every day. I don't want a single day to pass that you don't know how much I love you. I know how lucky I am to have you. I will never forget."

"I missed you too," I told him. I tried to hold back the tears, but I couldn't stop them.

"Come on, let's get in bed."

He took the bullet out of my hand and put it back in the drawer. He slipped me out of my clothes, pulled the comforter back, and helped me slide between the soft sheets before he quickly undressed and got in beside me. Levi pulled me close, his naked body hot as I pressed into him. I couldn't get close enough – skin on skin.

I cuddled in and ran my hand over his chest. "I don't want to talk about the past anymore, but I have to say, you look a whole lot different now than you did back then," I said, moving my hand over his stomach, enjoying the way his muscles tightened under my touch.

"Are you saying my penis grew?" he asked.

"No, you idiot." I slapped his stomach.

"Oh, you mean the sexy six-pack." He laughed.

Once again, I rolled my eyes. "Conceited much?"

"No baby, I'm not conceited. However, I see the way you look at me when I'm naked."

"Whatever."

"I'm kidding." He placed his hand over mine, halting my exploration. "I'm so happy you're here."

"Why did you ignore me in the car when I told you I loved watching you sing?"

He didn't speak for a long while, and I remained quiet, patiently waiting for an explanation, his thumb moving over my hand that rested on his stomach.

"Because it dawned on me after you said that I hadn't sung since I left you."

I was shocked. "Why not? You love music."

"No. I love the way you look at me when I sing to you. Your eyes light up, and all your attention is on me. There is no better feeling in the world. I love music because of what it does to you."

"You'll never stop singing again, Levi McCoy."

"Roger that, wife." He tugged my hand, moving me over him, and lifted his head to reach my mouth.

When his lips touched mine, all thoughts of singing flew out the window, and we proceeded to make a different kind of music, a perfect symphony of moans and grunts and a melody so sweet it brought tears to my eyes.

CHAPTER TWENTY-ONE

Levi

The commander took the news that I had married Blake better than I had thought. He only called me a "fucking idiot" half a dozen times before he said that if I knock her up, *his* words, before we got a lock on the oil company chatter he would cut my balls off.

Lenox, the bastard, laughed his ass off, probably happy the commander was no longer talking about his testicles in reference to the rate at which he was popping out kids. We needed the CIA's involvement with the op, and Blake was one of the best. She would be needed out in the field to go undercover.

As much as I wanted to start a family immediately, I also wanted some time alone with her, the two of us rediscovering each other. I didn't want to share her just yet – but soon.

The arrest warrant was ready, and Blake's change of command was official. She was now on loan from the CIA to the Army. She was practically bouncing with excitement as Jasper, Lenox, and Clark went over all the documents that she'd compiled. They'd combed through the evidence against Alister, double checking nothing was missing or incomplete. Of course, it was perfect.

We were ready to go up to Virginia and deliver the warrant. Grayson would be meeting us there to take Alister in.

"What's the play?" I asked Blake.

"I want to wait until he is home, knock on the door, and walk right in," she said.

Not that I minded her plan, but I did wonder about her reasoning. Taking him from the house also meant that my mother or sister might be present.

"Why the house?" I asked.

"Because I want this to end where it all started. In his study, where he tried to ruin me," she explained.

I understood her reasons. She needed the closure. I had not been back to the house since the day I packed my shit and left. That happened to be the same day I found Alister and Blake. After I had driven around for hours, I went back later that night and grabbed my stuff. I bounced around from friend's house to friend's house until it was time for me to leave for basic. Luckily, I didn't have that long to wait. I guessed that's why Alister had put the pressure on Blake. As the weeks went by and my ship date got closer, Alister and my mother were arguing with me more and more about changing my mind and going to college.

"Sounds good. Wheels up in thirty," I told her.

Four hours later I was standing in the perfectly manicured driveway of my stepfather's sixteen-thousand square foot mansion. The stone exterior with custom Tuscan-style columns boxing in the large front porch looked exactly like I had remembered. I knew the marble floors, cream wainscot paneling, and hella-expensive custom molding around the twenty-foot ceilings would still be as cold as they were the day I left. There was nothing warm and inviting about this house. It was not a home; it was a shrine to Alister and his over-inflated pompous ego. The eight-bedroom, ten-bathroom house complete with sauna, theater room, and tennis courts were all for show; a grand appearance for a man that was a cold-hearted killer. He might not be the one pulling the trigger, but he certainly was pulling the strings.

There were no cars in the driveway, but there never were. Alister said it looked classless to have vehicles parked on his imported brick drive, even if those vehicles were an Aston Martin, Mercedes, and a Porsche. They were to be parked in one of the five garage bays. One of the biggest fights we'd gotten into was not about the Army; it was over my pickup truck. He hated it, and that was all the more reason for me to keep it. My mother and sister were easily bought off and quickly ditched their used cars, a Honda and Toyota at the time, trading up to the Porsche and Merc. I refused to let my truck go. I bought it with money I had saved. That was the only fight Alister and I had where my mother took my side; on everything else she sided with him.

I hated this house. I hated what it did to my mom and how it destroyed my family. I would like to have said that I knew my mom and sister didn't know about what Alister was doing, but I couldn't. I didn't know either of them anymore. And if my mom could easily turn her back on her child there was no telling what she was capable of. Hell, a few months ago when her mother passed away, I was the only one that would handle the estate. I guess the measly fifty-thousand dollars my grandmother had left wasn't enough for my mother to be bothered with.

I saw a figure pass by the large front window. With the sheer white drapery, I couldn't make out if it was female or male. However, someone was home.

"Ready?" I asked.

"Hell, yes."

I watched as my brave wife marched her ass up the front steps and knocked on the door. I came up behind her and Grayson stood off to the side holding a briefcase with the warrant.

The door came open, and the man himself appeared.

Alister Bench.

Time had not been kind to him; he looked much older than his sixty years. At one time he had been a fit man and a commanding presence. Today, he looked pudgy and weak.

"Oh look, the prodigal son returns home, with his white-trash girlfriend," Alister sneered.

"Wife," I corrected.

"Of course you'd marry trash. After all, no matter how hard I tried I couldn't remove the stain of the ghetto off of you," he replied.

I wasn't going to take the bait. It no longer

mattered what this vile piece of shit said about Blake or me.

"May we come in?" Blake asked and smiled sweetly at him.

"Your mother isn't here, she's at the spa," Alister told me, guessing I wanted to see my mother.

"I'm here to talk to you."

Alister stepped aside to let us in and walked toward his study off the foyer. "I'd offer you a drink, but I don't have any Jack Daniels in the house. I don't want to waste my Dalmore on an Army private that wouldn't appreciate a single malt Scottish Whisky."

"First Sergeant," I corrected him again.

"Same difference. Army grunt. What do you want?" Coming to a stop in front of his desk, he turned to face Blake and me.

I glanced at Blake; she gave nothing away as she stood by my side, shoulders back, head held high, and a sly smile on her face.

Damn, she looked beautiful. I remained quiet and waited for Blake; this was her show. I was merely a bystander.

CHAPTER TWENTY-TWO

Blake

I hoped Alister couldn't see how badly I was shaking. Not out of fear, I was no longer afraid of this man. I was using all of my control not to strangle the arrogant bastard.

"I have a few questions about Muscat, Oman," I started.

"It is a filthy shit hole full of uneducated people. But you must know that Miss Porter seeing as you have visited the country many times. You were only in Yemen a few weeks ago, yes?" he asked.

"So, you've followed my career?" I smiled.

"If that's what you want to call it. Two-bit reporting for the Daily Sun. It is a shame really. I saw so much potential in you. I should've known better than to try and pluck trash out of the dumpster."

"You mean when you tried to blackmail me into leaving Levi and pay me off with an internship at one of your papers? I'm surprised that you'd consider dirtying up one of your media outlets with my presence."

"Yes, well, you can't blame me for trying. Madeline was beside herself with grief that her son was leaving. What would you like to know about Muscat? I don't make a habit of giving information to my competitors, but I will be buying up the Sun soon, so I suppose it won't hurt."

"I'm afraid you will not be buying anything, Mr. Bench. You see, where you will be going you'll be more concerned about not dropping the soap than mergers and acquisitions."

Alister smiled and threw his head back, laughing long and hard. I allowed this to continue for some time. It would make this next part so much more fun.

"I see you're still as naïve as you were at eighteen when you thought a silly voice recording was going to hurt my reputation. Once I acquire the Sun, your termination will be my first order of business. I refuse to have incompetent people working for me. Your days are numbered. You'll never get another job as a reporter when I'm done with you," he threatened.

"That is perfect, actually. You see for the last eight years it has been exhausting carrying out my duties and working the desk at the Daily Sun. I'm more than happy to give the cover up."

"The cover? What are you rambling on about?"

I pulled the leather identification wallet out of my pocket and opened it up and flashed it in Alister's direction.

"Alister Bench, you are under arrest," I announced.

"What the fuck are you talking about?" Alister huffed, leaning in looking at my credentials. "You can't arrest me, you idiot. That badge says CIA. You have no law enforcement function, nor do you have jurisdiction in the United States. Get out of my house," he yelled is face turning a nice shade of cranberry.

"You see Mr. Bench, the beauty of being good at my job is, unlike you, a lot of people in really high places like me. The Director of the FBI personally saw to it this afternoon that I was sworn in as a federal agent with all of the proper jurisdiction to arrest your arrogant ass. In about two minutes federal agents are going to swarm your pretty house and tear it apart. Under the Patriot Act, you're charged with twenty-three acts of funding known terror organizations. We will start there and work our way through more charges. Please turn around Mr. Bench. You have the right to remain..."

"Fuck you." He cut me off and started to go behind his desk.

"I really wouldn't do that, Mr. Bench." I sighed, pulling my .45 from under my blazer, leveling it in his direction.

"Did you really think I was going to let you take me in?" he asked and opened the top drawer.

"I don't much care how this ends, Bench. Only that you're stopped."

"Even if I make you a widow?" he asked and pointed the gun in Levi's direction.

The loud crack of gunfire echoed off the wood paneling in the room leaving my ears ringing.

I holstered my weapon and turned to look at Levi.

"Ready to go home?" he asked.

"Yes."

I heard Grayson chuckling behind us and the sirens as they pulled into the driveway. Not the most appropriate time to be laughing; there was a man dead bleeding on an expensive Persian rug. I didn't take pleasure in having to kill Alister Bench, but I wasn't going to lose sleep over it either. The man had been responsible for hundreds of deaths around the world.

I turned my attention away from the growing puddle of blood that pooled around Alister's body to my husband. Twelve years ago, I'd lost the man I loved standing in this very spot. When the door slammed that day, I thought my life had ended. Today, we would walk out that same door together. And when we closed the door behind us, it would not be the end of our story. Today, we would not be turning the page or ending a chapter of our lives.

Today we were starting a whole new book.

CHAPTER TWENTY-THREE

Nolan Clark

Holy sweet mother of God!

That was my first thought.

My second was holy fucking hell, that ass!

Sam Hunt's "Body Like a Back Road" was blasting on the stereo and all my intentions of busting Jasper's balls for playing chick music fled and were replaced with the aforementioned notions.

The sexy woman in front of me - who was currently in some bendy yoga-inspired pose - most certainly had the body that had inspired Sam Hunt to write the song.

Sweet Jesus. Those legs.

I wasn't one for going slow as the song suggested, but curves like those? They were made to explore –

slowly, diligently, and thoroughly. Toned, tanned legs like that were made to wrap around a man's waist and hold tight. An ass that was more than a handful - tight yet would still ripple as you took her from behind. Or maybe it wouldn't, and my overactive imagination and underused cock were just hoping that's what it'd do. God knows it would be a tragedy if it didn't.

The song changed, and the new singer crooned on about how he'll never settle down and how he doesn't dance. The woman in front of me straightened; her blonde hair pulled up in a knot on the top of her head, not giving me any indication how long it was but exposing a sexy tattoo on the back of her neck. Suddenly I felt like a dick for eye fucking the girl.

I cleared my throat, hoping to get her attention, but between the music and the amount of concentration it must've taken to balance on one leg the way she was, she hadn't heard me.

With both feet now planted firmly on the ground, she looked like she was getting ready to bend over again. I had to stop her. I was in a pair of athletic shorts that would, in no way, conceal a hard-on. And if she bent over in front of me again, I'd be able to pound nails with my cock.

I thought about just slipping out of the room and going across the lawn and knocking on Jasper's door. She'd never know I was here and I wouldn't have to bother her.

That's what I had planned to do until Jasper yelled my name from his deck and the woman turned and fell forward when she saw me.

"Whoa. Careful," I said and reached out my hand to steady her, catching her hips as she stumbled.

She turned, and I realized the first two thoughts I'd had about this woman did not do her justice. She was even more stunning from the front. Brownish-green eyes stared at me, wide and in shock. Her full lips were parted ever so slightly like she had been getting ready to say something. Beads of sweat dotted her impressive cleavage and disappeared down under her sports bra.

"I, um, didn't know... Sorry. You scared me," she stammered and pulled her hand out of mine.

Had I really been holding on to the poor girl's hand? What the hell was wrong with me? And why the fuck did I have the urge to grab her hand again? The brief contact wasn't enough; I wanted more.

"No need to apologize. I'm the one that's sorry. I

was looking for Jasper. I didn't mean to interrupt," I told her. "I'm Clark, by the way. I work with Jasper."

"Right. He's mentioned you. I'm Reagan. Nice to meet you."

Reagan.

Liz's little sister Reagan.

Well, fuck me. Totally and completely off limits.

"You, too. I'll let you get back to your work out."

It was difficult, but I didn't allow my eyes to move from her face. As desperate as I was for one more look, I didn't do it. Instead, I turned on my heels and hightailed it out of the too-small space like a pussy and nearly ran into Jasper.

"You ready?" I asked.

"Yeah. Let me see if Reagan is."

"Reagan?"

What the hell? Jasper and I were going to the boxing gym, did she need a ride somewhere?

"She's coming with us to work out."

"She is?"

"What the fuck is wrong with you? Did you forget how to speak, or are you having issues understanding the English language?"

I didn't know what my problem was. I'd never acted like a stuttering teenager around women, not even when I was a teenager.

"Do you think that's a good idea? The boxing gym this time of day is gonna be filled with nothing but meatheads. They're gonna trip over their dicks when she walks in looking like that."

Jasper threw his head back and roared with laughter. "Like you are?"

Fucker.

"Seriously. What the fuck are you thinking?"

"Good thing we'll both be there then. She'll have two big brother types to watch her back."

Big brother? Did he just say big brother? Because the last thing I was feeling toward Reagan was anything close to brotherly.

Reagan was quiet on the short drive to the gym. She sat in the back of my Jeep, content in her thoughts, while Jasper and I talked about the new training rotation we were starting today. I liked that she didn't need to be the center of attention but interjected when she had something thoughtful to say.

Where the hell had that come from? What did it matter what I liked? I shouldn't like anything about her.

The next two hours were torture. I was in hell. Every buffed-out gym-rat in the room couldn't keep their eyes off Reagan. Not that I could either, and more than that, I shouldn't have cared - but I did.

"Hey, Rea. Come jump in the ring with Clark while I get a drink," Jasper called ringside to where Reagan was standing, watching us now that she was done with her bag work.

I didn't know if Jasper was punishing me, or if this was his way of keeping Reagan away from the other men in the room. Her small frame slipped through the ropes easily, and all the impure thoughts I had earlier came rushing back with a vengeance. Not that they had been far from the forefront of my mind. Only now, my cock was being strangled by the cup I was wearing. What could I say? My dick had good taste, and Reagan looked positively edible.

"Sorry to intrude on your workout," Reagan said, coming to a stop in front of me.

She couldn't have been more than five feet three. I had almost a full foot on her in height and at least doubled her weight. She was a little thing; the words fun-sized popped into mind along with all the fun things I could do with her.

"You're not intruding. I hope you're not uncomfortable around all these idiots."

"They don't bother me. I'm kinda used to it. Back home, at my old gym, the guys either hit on me the entire time I was trying to work out, or they were offended I would dare enter a boxing gym and made it known women weren't wanted invading their space."

I didn't know why that pissed me off, but it did.

"What got you into boxing?" I asked.

I'd never met a woman that was interested in any sport where there was a good amount of blood involved.

"I don't want to tell you; you'll laugh," she said, tucking her head.

I wanted to touch her, lift her chin and make her look at me.

"Now you have to tell me. I won't laugh. Promise."

She raised her eyes to mine and twisted her lips. How fucking adorable was this girl? Adorable? What the hell was she doing to me? I didn't use words like adorable. I don't even think kittens or babies are adorable.

"When I was in high school, there was this boy, and I wanted to impress him, so I started boxing." She stopped and was trying her hardest to bite back a smile. She lost the battle and her face split into the most devastating smile I'd ever seen. "Sorry. I'm fucking with you. I couldn't keep a straight face, so I ruined it." She covered her mouth to hide her smile, and I wanted to demand she lower her hand and never hide from me again.

I chuckled when she continued to laugh behind her gloved hand.

"So, you know how to spar?" I asked.

She nodded her head.

"Do you want to go a round? Promise to pull my punches."

She stopped laughing and stood straight, steel infusing her spine as she stared me down.

"You better not. It'll piss me off if you do."

"Damn woman, I didn't mean to offend you, but you do realize I outweigh you by at least a hundred pounds, right? I'm not being sexist here; I'm being real."

"If you have to take it easy on me then I have no business being in the ring with you," she replied.

Someone had messed with her head if that's what she thought. Size mattered, especially in sparring. I was six feet two inches and two hundred pounds. I could hurt her in a matter of seconds if I wanted to, and not because of my training, simply because I was so much bigger than her.

"You know there are weight classes for a reason, right?" I asked.

"Do you think some man who finds me in a back alley is going to pull his punches or care that he outweighs me? Besides, weight classes are for sissies."

I didn't know her well enough to know if she was joking or not. On the one hand, I was impressed with her fire, on the other, I wanted to straighten out her line of thinking. But again, I didn't know her well, and it wasn't my place. And she was right, if someone trying to harm her they wouldn't go easy on her.

"Then call me a sissy and let's go a light round for points. Hands only?" I asked.

We both had sparring gloves on, but neither of us had on shin guards. Shin-on-shin contact hurt like a bitch, and it didn't matter how careful you were, it was inevitable.

"You're on," she answered, and took an open fighting stance.

One leg back, knees slightly bent, and an even, low center of gravity. Interesting, she'd had some martial arts training as well.

We'd danced around each other for a few minutes before I saw an opening. A quick one-two combination, I tapped her solar plex and waited for her to drop her hands in an effort to block my punch. When she did, I landed a jab to her cheek.

"Damn, you're quick," she said, shaking off my strike.

"That's a first," I laughed.

"What is?"

"Hearing a woman tell me I'm quick."

"Charming."

Her hands came back up, and she threw a wide, arching right hook. I easily ducked her attempt but was too late to block the snap of her round kick to my face. My neck snapped left, and I tasted blood.

Goddamn that was hot. What the hell was wrong with me?

"Shit, sorry. I didn't mean to do that. You said hands only."

I straightened to my full height and looked down at Reagan. Her hair was a matted, sweaty mess, her face was red and blotchy from exertion, and with all that, she had to have been the sexiest woman I'd ever laid eyes on. I couldn't stop myself from wondering if this was what she looked like after sex.

"Now you owe me dinner," I told her.

"What?" She laughed. "Why would I owe you dinner?"

"The first to draw blood has to buy the other person dinner."

"Is that a rule?" She'd stopped dancing around and was fidgeting with her glove.

"It is now."

I knew I had no business flirting with Reagan. I certainly had no business going out to dinner with her. Yet, I absolutely was going to do it. Maybe after I spent some time with her, she'd do something or say something that would show her true colors. All women did. With some it took an hour, with others, it took days, or in my ex-wife's case, it took years. But sooner or later the pretense fades.

That's what I needed.

Once she showed me who she really was, I'd be able to stop this weird fascination I seemed to have.

It was only a matter of time.

NOLAN CLARK IS the last man standing. While he is happy his teammates have found love, he's even happier to be single. But fate is a funny thing.

Freedom is up next... grab your copy now.

Nightstalker

Protecting Olivia

Redeeming Violet

Recovering Ivy

Rescuing Erin

The Gold Team - Susan Stoker Universe

Brooks

Thaddeus

Kyle

Maximus

Declan

Blue Team - Susan Stoker Universe

Owen

Gabe

Myles

Kevin

Cooper

Garrett

The 707 Freedom Series

Free

Freeing Jasper

Finally Free

Freedom

The Next Generation (707 spinoff)

Saving Meadow

Chasing Honor

Finding Mercy

Claiming Tuesday

Adoring Delaney

Keeping Quinn

Taking Liberty

Triple Canopy

Damaged

Flawed

Imperfect

Tarnished

Tainted

Conquered

Shattered

Fractured

The Collective

Unbroken

Trust

Standalones

Romancing Rayne

Falling for the Delta Co-written with Susan Stoker

BE A REBEL

Riley Edwards is a USA Today and WSJ bestselling author, wife, and military mom. Riley was born and raised in Los Angeles but now resides on the east coast with her fantastic husband and children.

Riley writes heart-stopping romance with sexy alpha heroes and even stronger heroines. Riley's favorite genres to write are romantic suspense and military romance.

Don't forget to sign up for Riley's newsletter and never miss another release, sale, or exclusive bonus material.

Rebels Newsletter

Facebook Fan Group

www.rileyedwardsromance.com

facebook.com/Novelist.Riley.Edwards

instagram.com/rileyedwardsromance

bookbub.com/authors/riley-edwards

amazon.com/author/rileyedwards

www.ingramcontent.com/pod-product-compliance
Lightning Source LLC
Chambersburg PA
CBHW070500200726
48293CB00007B/2308